Drive-by Psychosis

Drive-by Psychosis

Catherine Hilterbrant

iUniverse LLC
Bloomington

Drive-by Psychosis

iUniverse books may be ordered through booksellers or by contacting:

iUniverse LLC
1663 Liberty Drive
Bloomington, IN 47403
www.iuniverse.com
1-800-Authors (1-800-288-4677)

ISBN: 978-1-4697-7835-8 (sc)
ISBN: 978-1-4697-7836-5 (e)

Printed in the United States of America

iUniverse rev. date: 12/13/2013

CHAPTER ONE

Linda Cresswood stares up at the ceiling while lying on her soft, comfortable bed. Her room is well organized and clean. Drawings, paintings, band posters, and pictures full of family and friends fill her walls. She has a stereo and many CDs containing all genres of music. She wonders what she is going to do with her life. *I can't believe that I just graduated from Parkview High and that I'm going to Century State University in September. How am I going to deal with getting an apartment, paying bills, and getting a new job?* She quit her job at Puddy's Coffee House last week because the boss was a jerk.

Linda's appearance is unique. She has a light-brown, punk-inspired haircut, which looks feminine and alluring. Her skin is a light golden brown, blessed without imperfections. She wears laid-back clothes most of the time, but she can dress in a sophisticated way if she wants or needs to. She is long and lean, about five-seven. She can wear anything since she has such a good figure. People always say she has model looks, but appearances are not a big deal for her; she prefers to use her brain. She lives in a two-story house with three bedrooms and baths on Tomlin Street in a town called Josewood. Her house has a manicured lawn, a gigantic pool, and the latest fashion in furniture and entertainment. What can you say? She is lucky to be a rich kid. She lives with her parents and a brother named David, whom Linda calls "The Devil" Cresswood. He is two years younger than her and is going into his junior year at Parkview High. David has dark brown hair and good genes, which is why he is so popular with the girls. He has green eyes like Linda. He is muscular and in shape, since he works out at the local gym. He is five-eight, with a face that can melt the coldest of ice queens. David is smart, athletic, and handsome. He is the total package for any girl.

Linda goes downstairs to make herself a sandwich. It is a warm day, perfect for swimming. *I love summer because it has a serene quality to it,* Linda thinks. A thought then bursts into her head. *What I need is a road trip with my best friends*. She turns to grab the phone on the counter when David jumps from behind the counter and shouts, "*Raawwrr*!" David has a tendency to do annoying things.

"Dammit, David, you scared the shit out of me, you stupid loser!" Linda says as she catches her breath.

"Aww, is the little baby gonna cry?" David remarks.

"Shut up!" Linda yells as she slaps him upside his head.

"Feisty little thing, aren't you? Just watch the hair," David says as he looks at one of his pocket mirrors. He walks outside.

Why does he care? Linda thinks. His hair is medium short and messy, but in a fashionable way.

Linda picks up the phone and calls Samantha. Linda and Samantha Deroux have been friends since fifth grade at Pollywog Elementary. Samantha is blonde, five-six, and has fair, silky skin and a knockout figure. Samantha really likes sports. This helps her maintain her physique. Her eyes are a dark gray, which always reminds Linda of stormy weather.

"Hello?" Samantha speaks into the phone.

Linda replies, "Oh, hi. Sammy, it's me. Linda. I was wondering if you wanted to go on a road trip with me." Then there is silence.

"You're one random girl, but I got nothing else to do. Let me check with my parents," says Samantha. Linda waits.

"Yeah, it's okay, as long as I call them on the road. Whose car are we taking?" asks Samantha.

"Mine. So what are you doing right now, Sammy?" asks Linda.

"Just installing a bigger TV. It's like I'm at the movies now," replies Samantha.

"You're the luckiest son of a bitch I know." Linda laughs. She is envious that Samantha is an only child, because she gets anything she asks for. "Love ya, Sams, we'll talk later. Oh, and I'm thinking of bringing the rest of the bunch too."

"Okay, just make sure that the car won't be too cramped," Samantha says.

"No problem. Bye," says Linda as she hangs up the phone. She calls the others, Jennifer, Josh, and Eric. All of their parents agree. Linda's eighteenth birthday is coming up and she likes the idea of celebrating it on the road.

Linda's parents, Tammy and George Cresswood, walk through the door. Tammy has dark brown hair and green eyes. She is five-nine. George has light brown hair and brown eyes. He is six feet tall. They both have a light golden skin tone.

"Mom? Dad? Can I go on a road trip three days from now?" asks Linda.

The sudden request surprises them. "Who? What? When and where is this going to take place?" Tammy asks.

"I want to go with my friends on Interstate 6 up the coast," Linda says.

"How are you going to pay for this trip?" George asks.

"I was thinking that everyone would split expenses and that I can use my money from my last paycheck. Please, it's going to be my birthday," Linda says.

George replies, "Well, if that's what you want . . . okay."

Tammy thoughtfully looks at Linda and says, "Well, you are old enough. I will talk to the other parents to get things situated."

Linda smiles and hugs her parents. "Thank you so much."

Linda goes back to her room to change into her bathing suit. She wants to go swimming in her pool. David is sun bathing in a lounge chair when she arrives at the pool. "What are you so happy about?" David asks as he sees her smiling face.

"I'm going on a road trip and you're not invited. *Na-na-na-na-na,*" teases Linda.

"What? They actually let you go?" asks David in a surprised tone.

"Yes, as long as I keep in contact with them daily," Linda says.

"Well, I'll be partying," David says nonchalantly as he resumes his sun bathing.

"Whatever," says Linda. She makes a perfect dive into the pool. The water is refreshing. It's a perfect temperature to swim in. As she is practicing her swim strokes, she keeps thinking about the trip. *I can't wait for it to begin. I need a relaxing vacation to keep my mind away from the major responsibilities of growing up.* She is going to use her car during the drive because it has the best gas mileage out of all her other friends' cars. *Now, what am I going to put in my suitcase?*

Chapter Two

The next day Linda calls Samantha and the rest of her friends. Three days later, she picks up each of them from their doorsteps. Everyone greets each other with enthusiastic hugs and hellos. They get themselves comfortable in the car while Linda takes the on-ramp to Interstate 6. Josh has the map. He looks at it and asks, "What's the first stop?"

"Any place eighty miles from here," Linda replies.

"What if I have to pee?" Jennifer asks.

"Of course we'll have rest stops along the way," Samantha replies.

"What's the name of the town, Josh?" Linda asks.

"Ryeman," says Josh.

"What a weird name," says Jennifer. Linda asks if everyone brought his or her share of the money. They all did. An hour and a half later, they arrive at Ryeman. It is a busy town with shops and eateries. It is about 9:30 a.m.

They pick the cheapest hotel to save money. Their room has two king-sized beds and it is on the top floor of the three-story hotel. They begin to unpack. "I'm hungry. Let's eat some breakfast," Eric says. Eric Onen has short, dark blond hair. He was a star athlete in soccer and a straight-A student in Parkview High School, which is why he got a full scholarship to Parmay University. He didn't need the money since he comes from an affluent family, but they gave it to him anyway. He is muscular and well defined in a natural way. He is five-eight, with hazel eyes. His face is flawless and he has a great smile. He is sensitive but strong and always has a long list of girls' numbers.

"What restaurant are we going to?" Samantha asks. They all get back into the car and look for a place to eat a couple of blocks from the hotel. They go to Edna's Diner. Eric orders ham, bacon, and eggs. Jennifer orders waffles. Josh orders ham and hash browns. Samantha and Linda order chocolate pancakes.

"These are the best damn waffles I ever ate in my life," says Jennifer.

About an hour later, everyone finishes breakfast. "I'm stuffed," says Josh.

"Me too," says Eric.

"Chocolate pancakes are always delicious," Samantha says. Linda agrees. They pay the cashier and leave the waiter a tip. When they leave the restaurant, the weather has warmed up to about seventy-eight degrees.

"Let's walk around to digest our food," says Jennifer. They agree and go into a store called Sanquo. While Samantha, Eric, and Jennifer are looking for clothes, Josh walks up to Linda and says, "So, do you like the trip so far?"

"It's okay," Linda replies.

"Can you believe that high school is over?" asks Josh.

"Yeah, I know. Thank God. A bunch of fake-ass people anyway," says Linda. They both laugh.

"Are you going to buy some clothes?" Josh asks.

"Maybe, if something interests me," Linda replies.

"Linda? Is this shirt cute? Come over here," Jennifer calls from a few clothes racks behind them.

"Gotta go, Josh," says Linda.

Josh Agoldin is muscular, five-eight, and also has a nice smile. He has olive skin and handsome features. He has dark brown eyes and short, wavy brown hair. He is very bright and talented. He plays the guitar, drums, and bass. He also has the qualities of a gentleman. Many girls get entranced when looking at him. Linda met him when they were both freshmen at Parkview High. Josh has been best friends with Eric since middle school, so that is how she also met Eric. Eric calls for Josh to check out some bargains on some pants. He is holding a pair of discounted designer jeans.

Linda looks at the top that Jennifer wants. It is very artistic, with abstract pictures such as birds and garbage cans. "Yeah, it's cute," says Linda. She looks at the price tag. "And it's a good deal."

"I know," Jennifer says happily. Jennifer Corali is five-six, with dark-brown straight hair and blue eyes. She has a sun-kissed complexion and perfect skin. Everything about her face is beautiful. Her blue eyes are sometimes distracting. She also has a perfect figure that went well with any kind of clothes she bought. She met Linda when she was in elementary school.

Samantha walks over with a pair of flats. "Aren't these beautiful?" she asks. They have different cartoons printed on them.

"Wow, this is a nice place to shop," says Linda.

Josh buys a trucker hat and a graphic belt. Linda buys some chandelier earrings. Everyone finishes paying and walks back to the car. "Where do you guys want to go?" asks Linda.

"How about a park? We can rest in the shade," suggests Samantha.

"That's a good idea," agrees Jennifer.

"That sounds boring," says Eric.

"No, it doesn't. It sounds rather relaxing," says Josh.

"Stop kissing ass," retorts Eric.

"Shut up," says Josh as he playfully punches him in the arm.

Linda sees a park after driving ten miles from the restaurant. The sign reads McPhillips Park. Linda parks her car and gets a blanket out of the trunk. She lays it down on a nice shady spot, thanks to a big oak tree.

CHAPTER THREE

Everyone sits down and starts talking. After a while, Linda feels like she wants to walk. "Does anyone want to take a walk with me?"

"I'm tired," says Jennifer.

"So am I," agrees Samantha.

"Me too," adds Eric.

"I'll go with you," says Josh.

"Okay," says Linda. The others are being lazy. Josh and Linda walk on a path through the well-maintained park. The path is bordered with rosebushes. Josh is the first to speak. "It's a nice day."

"It is. It's better being outside than indoors," Linda says.

"We're growing up, you know," says Josh in a playful tone.

"Don't remind me. I have enough to think about," retorts Linda sarcastically. There is a bench up ahead of them. "Do you want to sit down over there?"

Josh looks to where she is pointing. "Okay." says Josh. They sit down. "I like being on the road 'cause I feel like I don't have to worry about life problems," he says.

"That's true," agrees Linda.

"I'm really glad you thought this up. I think everyone needed this," says Josh.

"Yeah, I know. I'm glad my parents and everyone else agreed to it."

"Your birthday is coming up," says Josh.

"Yes, very soon," says Linda.

"Don't worry, Linda, we all planned something very special for you."

"Really? That's great!" she exclaims.

"You're an amazing person; that's why you deserve it," says Josh. He gets up and walks back to the group. Linda sits on the bench with a puzzled look on her face.

Everyone decides after spending the night that it is time to leave Ryeman. Eric goes to the hotel office to check out. Linda and the rest of the group are waiting in the car. Eric hops in the front seat. "Where do we go now?" asks Linda.

"Let's continue taking Interstate 6; maybe there might be a better town," suggests Samantha.

"That sounds like a good idea," says Josh.

"I agree; that's the best decision," says Eric imitating a Scottish accent. Everyone laughs.

"Shut up," says Linda playfully.

After two hours, twenty rest stops, and five pounds of junk food, they arrive in a lively town called Thompson. "We're finally here. After all that gasoline-wasting time, we've actually arrived somewhere nice," says Linda. She drives down Zan Boulevard and checks into The Morning Star Hotel. While everyone is unpacking his or her stuff in the hotel room, Linda thinks of the finances of the trip, but something else distracts her and she forgets all about it. Samantha walks over to Linda and says, "Let's look at the shops,"

"Okay," Linda replies.

"Do you guys want to go shopping with us?" asks Samantha.

"I'm bored of shopping," replies Josh.

"Me too," says Eric. They preferred to do guy stuff.

"I'm going to call my mom, then swim in the pool and work on my tan," says Jennifer. They agree to go their separate ways.

The world is beautiful. Life is full of so many adventures, so much beauty to absorb. I want to breathe in its history. I want nature to possess me again. It is beaten out of us since the day we are born. That is what civilization and society do. They beat out creativity, freedom of spirit, your inner child, and happiness. People are now like puppets, afraid to show their true selves in fear that they will be ridiculed and unwanted. They are slaves to the dictators of society. They are a kind of people that only follow. They try so hard to be what others say is acceptable. Why would you let your lives be controlled? As soon as you let that happen, your life ceases to be your own; it belongs to someone else. You become mindless and heartless: in other words, a robot. Linda thinks about this as she walks with Samantha toward the shops.

Linda does not want to buy anything. She wants to kill time with her best friend. They see a drug-addled mentally unstable man yelling at himself across the street. The cops are trying to get him to calm down. He does not; instead he gets violent. They quickly pin him down, cuff him, and throw him into the back seat of the patrol car. What is comic about life is that it consists of tragedy and laughter. There are drug addicts, drug dealers, prostitutes, rapists, and murderers. Then there are the homeless whose afflictions remain unheard of by those who have everything they lack. Then there are the successful rich whose materialistic, wasteful greed spreads like an infection. The middle class, who just want to live a steady and comfortable life, but who look furtively over their shoulders in fear of being stalked by destitution. Then there are those who want a happy life. That costs nothing. You can take two roads. Each one consists of good or evil. Here is one planet with two worlds.

"I want to get some sneakers," says Samantha.

Linda wakes up from her analysis on life. "What?"

"I said I want to buy some sneakers." Samantha does not even care about the commotion that happened across the street. "Shoes that look avant-garde."

They find a shoe store called Mellows. Linda cannot believe all the different styles they have just for tennis shoes. They also have many heels, flats, and sandals. This is a shoe fetishist's gold mine.

"Remember to save some money. You still have to eat and help with the hotel funds," says Linda.

"Yeah, I know. I'm not dumb," Samantha replies playfully.

Linda does not know why she is so money-conscious. She came from a rich family. Maybe it is because so many business folk are involved in her life. Her parents made their living from their businesses. Her mother and father are both CEOs. Mom ran a clothing mega-store, and her father, a popular fast-food corporation. She grew up being told to be smart with her money and make smart decisions. *I guess I feel thankful for that. I don't want to be irresponsible or stupid. I'm glad I have some sort of business sense.*

"Look, Lynn," Samantha shows her some high tops with graphics that look like graffiti. There are a lot of neon colors on it.

"Do you like it?" Linda asks.

"Yeah," replies Samantha.

"Then buy it," Linda says.

Samantha sits down on one of the benches. "I'm going to try them on . . . yeah, they fit. That's awesome," Samantha says while she giggles. They pay for the shoes at the cash register and leave the store.

Linda has an idea. *Samantha, Jennifer, and me should see a movie together. Oh yeah, my eighteenth birthday is coming up too. I wonder how they are going to surprise me.* "Do you want to go to the movies? We could take Jennifer along too," says Linda.

"Yeah, that's a great idea. I'm going to call Jennifer right now to see if she wants to go," says Samantha.

They walk back to the car. Linda needs to fill up her tank. *I'll do that on the way back to the hotel.*

"Yeah, she wants to go," Samantha reports as she hangs up her cell.

"What should we see, an action, comedy, or horror flick?" asks Linda.

"I hate horror movies. Let's see an action movie," says Samantha.

"Yeah, that sounds like the best," says Linda.

When they arrive back at the hotel, Jennifer's skin had tanned to a beautiful golden brown. She has just taken a shower.

"Hey, Jennifer, we decided to see an action film," says Linda.

"Great, that way it won't be boring," Jennifer says as she laughs. Jennifer always looks beautiful, even now, when she has no makeup and wet hair. "Let me put on my evening outfit.

"Your evening outfit?" asks Samantha.

"Yes, I brought clothes and shoes for different occasions," replies Jennifer, in a way that sounded like everyone did this.

"You are so high maintenance!" Linda laughs back as she playfully throws a pillow at Jennifer.

"Why shouldn't I be?" Jennifer laughs in response.

She gets her stuff and goes into the bathroom to change. Linda looks in the phone book to find a movie theater close to the hotel. After a couple of minutes, she finds an address and writes it down. Samantha fixes her hair in the mirror. Jennifer comes out wearing some high-end casual clothes. She uses the hotel blow dryer to style her hair. Linda is touching up her makeup and fixing her hair. In about thirty minutes, they are on their way to the movies. They find the movie theater by asking directions from locals. They decide to see a movie called *Major Destruction.* It is about a framed person who worked for the CIA. He has to catch certain criminals in order to clear his name. It has the same premise of every damn action movie.

People spend money to be distracted from the real world. They want to be entertained.

Chapter Four

I love you so much that I . . .
Woke you up and opened your eyes.
And by doing this I caused pain when I exposed you
to the life that you really lived. Even though you are
now broken, in despair and hesitant, I will restore and
love you until the day you decide to walk away.
Al' aan enta hur, habibi. (Now, you're free my love.)

The movie ends and the girls walk back into the cool night air. Samantha yawns, stretches, and says, "So what do you guys want to do now?"

"I don't know," replies Linda.

"Why don't we get something to eat?" asks Jennifer.

"That's a good idea 'cause I'm kinda hungry," says Samantha.

"Me too," agrees Linda. "Where are we going to eat?"

"Let's look around. There has got to be a place around here. We're next to a freaking movie theater!" says Jennifer. They walk past the movie theater. It did not take long to find a place to eat. They find a typical burger place that begs attention from youth profit. They head in that direction.

Jennifer begins to get lost in thought. *What will life look like if you are constantly on LSD for a week? What will you see? What will you remember? What will you do? Will you unconsciously kill yourself? Will you harm someone else?*

Samantha looks at the streets. Her mind is in deep thought. *What was the price for individuality? What was the price to think differently? What was the price to decide your own path in life? Why are people so scared of change? Why do we isolate ourselves in small circles? Why do we fight modernity and antiquity? What is it that scares us so much?*

Linda looks at the stars. *They are always so bright. I wonder what it would feel like to suffocate in space and die with the planets as witnesses. What do moon rocks taste like? What did pain feel like when a big black hole was sucking you in? I want to watch the earth, my habitat, spin on its axis. I want to have a front row seat of watching a star go supernova, without it hurting me, of course.*

The girls arrive at the restaurant entrance and walk inside. They wait in line. When it is their turn, they tell the cashier what they want. They all chip in money and pay the cashier. They sit down at one of the empty booths.

"So how do you like the night?" asks Jennifer.

"It's better than staying at the hotel," says Linda.

"Definitely," agrees Samantha.

Chapter Five

You're my comrade, so . . .
Your intentions must be worthy, or . . .
Someone might find your body.

The guys are finally away from the girls and free to do what they want. Eric and Josh decide to play some pool. They walk to a pool house and go inside. They begin to play.

"Yeah, right, when it's my turn again things will change," says Eric.

"That's what you said the last hundred times," replies Josh.

"Ha, ha. Very funny," retorts Eric in a sarcastic tone. They play for about an hour. Eric gets the upper hand and wins the game.

"That was a nice eight ball in the corner pocket," says Josh.

"Thanks," says Eric.

"You want to get something to drink?" asks Josh.

"Why don't we get something to eat along with it?"

"You're right," says Josh. They walk out of the pool house and down the block in hopes of finding a place to eat.

"Hey look, there's a place," says Eric.

"What kind of a place is it?" asks Josh.

"It's a restaurant, but they have a takeout option."

"Okay, let's go inside and order," says Eric. He orders some salmon with veggies, mashed potatoes on the side, and some iced tea. Josh orders a steak with the same side orders along with some soda. They take their meal and begin walking down the street. They decide to eat their meal at an empty bus stop.

"So what are we going to do now?" asks Eric as he pauses to eat his mashed potatoes.

"I don't know; we should do something crazy," replies Josh as he tries to cut his steak with a cheap, flimsy plastic knife.

"Hey, why don't we pick up some whores?" asks Eric.

"Are you trying to get us a venereal disease?" Josh demands of Eric, with a laugh.

"Well then, what do you want to do?" asks Eric.

"Why don't we go pick up some drunk girls at a bar?" asks Josh.

"Okay," says Eric.

"I think I saw a bar down the street," says Josh. They finish their meals and throw it away. They begin to walk down the street. Josh breathes in the air. *Life is beautiful. I want to live and breathe the city. There are so many people, millions of relationships to have and millions of things to do. What protects you from wickedness? Is life a balancing act between death and catastrophe? Or is it between delight and pain? What keeps us from getting hurt? Are we always a second away from death? I want to go to a sacred beach and sleep there for eternity without becoming a victim of robbery, attacks, or arrest. I want to go swimming in a clear turquoise ocean without getting my limbs eaten off by an ocean creature. I want to be served a variety of foods and drinks. I want to forget about all the dismal things that haunt and ruin my life. The stuff that creates guilt, that scares you into wanting to die to finally have peace and be able to get away.*

Eric looks at a plastic bag blowing in the street. *What will it feel like to drip honey on a woman and then lick her everywhere? What will happen if the planet ran out of air and we couldn't breathe? What will happen if lightning struck me? What would it feel like if public transportation ran me over? I wish my thoughts would just leave me alone. Most of the time, they make me feel worthless and ugly. They make me feel as if I have some sort of disgusting mental disease. I do not trust my brain because it is trying to destroy me. But, at the same time, it is trying to help me.*

When they arrive at the bar, they decide to wait outside. Eric takes out a pack of cigarettes and offers one to Josh. They both light up. Eric and Josh do not smoke often, just occasionally. They pass the time by chewing on mints and talking about insignificant stuff. After about twelve minutes, they see a couple of blondes walking out. They are young, in their twenties. They are laughing. One of the blondes looks flirtatiously at Eric. Both of the blondes walk over to them.

"Hi, are you guys enjoying the night?" asks the blonde with dark roots.

"Yes, and I suppose you as well?" asks Josh.

"Yes, we are, but I think my friend's a little drunk," interrupts the other blonde. "My name is Penelope, and this one is Daniela."

"I'm not a 'this one'," says the dark-rooted girl named Daniela. Penelope laughs. It is obvious to Eric and Josh that both of these girls are drunk.

"Hey, what's your name?" asks Penelope.

"My name is Josh, and this is my friend, Eric."

"Hey," greets Eric.

"You guys are really cute, do you want to hang out with us?" asks Penelope.

"Yeah, stay with us. You guys are really cute," says Daniela.

"Okay," says Josh. They all start walking away from the bar.

"Do you guys live around here?" asks Daniela.

"No, we're on vacation," says Eric.

"That's interesting," says Penelope. While they are walking, they come across a poorly lit playground. They sit down on some benches. The guys see that Penelope is whispering to Daniela. Daniela then looks at Eric. She smiles and says, "My friend says that she wants to talk to you."

"Okay," says Eric. There is a pause in the air.

"No . . . alone," Daniela turns to Josh. "I want to talk with you too." They each split up, but not too far off.

"So how's your night been going so far?" asks Daniela.

"All right, and yours?" asks Eric.

"Perfect. You know what? I don't even know you, but I feel like kissing you," says Daniela.

"What's preventing you?" asks Eric.

"I don't know, you could be a murderer," replies Daniela.

"If I were a murderer, I would have already killed you. However, if I was would that prevent you from kissing me?" asks Eric.

"Yes, but your face is too hard to resist," says Daniela as she lightly kisses him. Eric and Daniela begin to make out.

"You have a beautiful face," says Eric.

"Thanks."

As he kisses her, she takes off her skirt. Eric makes his move. His hands begin to feel her inner thighs. Her skin is soft, yes, but she smells like a whore. She brings him closer, as she removes her shirt. There she lies, on a bench hidden by trees with only a bra, panties, and darkness. His hand rests on her stomach, as he tastes her saliva. Slowly, his hand begins to drop down and then lower. His hand lightly grabs her vagina. Daniela begins to breathe hard. His hand then slides underneath her underwear.

She waxes, Eric thinks. His fingers begin to lightly play with the folds of her vagina. She lets out a whimper. He then inserts his finger into her vagina. It sucks and squeezes at his finger every time he slides it in and out of her. He removes his hand from her underwear.

"Turn over," says Eric.

"Why?" asks Daniela.

He gets close to her face and whispers in her ear in a sexy, but soothing way. "I want to fuck you from behind," whispers Eric.

"Kinky," purrs Daniela. She removes her bra and underwear. She turns over, gets on all fours and widens her knees a little. Eric unzips and pulls down his pants. He takes out a fresh packaged condom from his wallet and puts it on. He then positions himself behind her. He grabs her hips as he enters inside her. His penis pounds into her vagina as he pulls her hair and grabs her breasts. Daniela moans in pleasure. Eric stops.

"Your vagina feels kinda loose," says Eric.

"What the fuck did you say?" Daniela says in an annoyed tone as she turns around to look at him.

"Don't get mad, I'm just letting you know," says Eric.

"Fine, whatever. I'll tighten up my thighs, maybe that will fix it," Daniela retorts.

The sex is hard and fast. She has her orgasm before he does. Eric throws the condom away in the trash. He then pulls up his pants. He kisses her on the lips. "You were all right," he says.

"You surprisingly know how to fuck well. I wasn't really expecting much," says Daniela. Eric says nothing, he just laughs.

Across the darkness, somewhere else sit Josh and Penelope. "It's a nice night," says Josh.

"Yes, it is," says Penelope.

"You know, you're very beautiful," says Josh.

"You're just saying that," replies Penelope, blushing.

"No, for real," says Josh.

"Well, I think you're really good-looking, too," replies Penelope. Then there is silence.

"Are you cold?" Josh asks.

"Yes, a little," says Penelope. He moves closer and puts his arm around her.

"How about now?" asks Josh.

"Much better," says Penelope.

"Let me look at your eyes," says Josh.

"Why?"

"Because I like them." She turns to face him. He holds her chin with his hand. Her eyes are amber. "You have nice facial features," says Josh. He caresses the side of her cheek. Josh moves in closer and they kiss. Her mouth smells and tastes of alcohol, but her lips are eager. His hands are on her waist but they slowly slide upward. She begins to unbutton her blouse, but stops to kiss him some more. Josh finishes unbuttoning the rest. His hands move back down to caress her stomach. He can feel her skin heating up. He slowly unhooks her bra and removes it. Her breasts are small, delicate, but big enough to grab. As he kisses her, his hands move up from her side. When his hands arrive at her breasts, he begins to gently massage them. His thumbs move side to side across her nipples. She shudders lightly. She kisses his neck. He kisses her and starts to kiss lower. He kisses the top of her nipples and licks all the areas of her breasts. He looks at her. She looks at him with eyes of wanting more. He starts to suck her nipples, and they become hard in his mouth. She lets out a low, quick sigh of pleasure. He gives her nipples a light, gentle nibble when he finishes. He takes off her pants and then uses his teeth to take off her thong. He removes his pants and underwear. He finds a new condom in his wallet and puts it on. He gets between her thighs. She parts her legs enough for him. He shoves his dick intensely and deep into her vagina. She gasps. He thrusts his penis deep inside of her faster and faster. He doesn't even kiss her once while he is fucking her. She starts to moan a little louder.

"Shut up! Your stupid moaning is going to wake the whole neighborhood up," says Josh in a low voice.

"Don't tell me to shut up, you fucking asshole," says Penelope, but she quiets herself down anyway.

Josh fucks her until she has her orgasm and he ejaculates. He slides out of her, removes his condom, and throws it in a nearby trashcan. He gives her a kiss on the forehead. "It was okay," says Josh as he pulls his pants up.

As Penelope puts on her clothes, she is still breathing heavily. "It was nothing romantic, but I never had a guy make me orgasm that quickly," says Penelope.

Josh looks at her with a smirk. "Now you got one," says Josh. Josh signals to Eric that it is time to go. "I had a really nice time with you," says Josh.

"So did I," says Penelope. She puts her clothes back on. "Can you walk us to our car?" she asks.

"Sure," says Josh. They walk the girls over to their car while talking and laughing about different things. When they arrive at the car, they hug Penelope and Daniela, but in their hearts Josh and Eric feel nothing for these strange girls. They say their goodbyes. Josh and Eric watch them drive off.

Drunk driving. Maybe Eric and me should have made them take a cab. But you know what? I don't care what happens to them. If they cause an accident and kill someone else that's on their conscience, not mine. I'm not their keeper. Josh looks up at the sky and says, "That reminds me. I need to brush my teeth and take a shower."

Eric laughs and replies, "So do I."

Chapter Six

I need you to know.

Hey, I see you. Let's take a break. Let's cut the scene. Do you think you can look into people's lives and not expect someone to know that you are watching? I feel your eyes registering every line and its information to discover more and more about our malfunctions. You must be so eager for entertainment. If you are wondering who I am, I am nobody. I exist solely in the context of this story. I will not tell you who I am. That part is unnecessary. If you want to stay, stay. You are the only one who I will get to talk to before they dismantle me. Read what I feel. Read the fragments of me. So what is the real purpose of this world? What do I mean to you? What do I mean to anything? Sex is a survival tool for our species. We need to reproduce in order to keep our species going. Is that all we are? A competitive breed designed to eliminate competition either by numbers or by force. Does that mean all the emotions we feel are a lie? What if all our emotions are preprogrammed to make us fulfill the job to reproduce and destroy? Is the pleasure an incentive to make sure we produce more and more drones for our species? Is that all I am? Is that all you are? Born to wipe out someone or something's existence? Constantly creating and enlarging an army of the human species. Does that mean animals have their own army, too? What happens if we involve plants? Are we just on one huge battleground? If I am a killing machine, then I will complete my design and not let you survive. I always liked rain. I feel like the rain understands all my pain and everything I cannot describe with words. I feel it knows me more than I know myself. The sky turns black; it opens up and sucks me through. I leave my house. I leave my world. I leave my existence. I see you in a dream. You are so beautiful. I want to grab you. I want to breathe you in. I want to rip your heart out and eat it. I want to taste you from the inside. Life is rushing past me. I feel so dizzy. All my tears turn into gold. All my pain turns into heaven, and all my exhilaration into lavish gardens. I am one with the universe.

Chapter Seven

Run away with me or away from me.
The night is my lover.
The day is my commitment.
I cease to be human; I become the world.
You are my witness. You are my other half.

While the girls and Linda are having their night snack at the fast food joint, Linda looks out of the window and begins to daydream. *Growing up and trying to adapt to a fast-paced life is an uncomfortable transition for me. I want to explore the world before city life damages my brain. I do not want to be myself anymore. I want to reincarnate repeatedly so I can view life in its many perspectives. I want to set my soul free. I want to feel transcendent. I want to live, love, and be myself. I want everything that life can offer. I want everything. I want to be one with the earth again. I want to be on the highest mountain peaks and shout out my dreams, desires, and fears. I'm being so over-dramatic!* Linda thinks.

"Did you like the movie, Linda?" asks Samantha as she bites into her sandwich. Linda is eating soup; Jennifer is having a salad.

I love my friends. I love helping them out and listening to them, but the whole time that they are here next to me I want to transport to another world, thinks Linda. She stares out the huge window and sees how the darkness covers the streets.

They arrive back to the hotel at 12:00 a.m. The girls decide to call their parents to let them know where they are and that they are okay. If they did not call them, their parents would call their cell phones nonstop. Good parents worry like that. The girls take their separate showers and get in their pajamas. They turn on the TV and watch some comedy. The guys did not get back until one in the morning. They came stumbling in and laughing. "Where have you guys been?" asks Samantha.

"Just doing mischief," says Eric.

"Yeah," says Josh.

"You guys should call your parents to let them know you're okay," says Jennifer.

"We are so ahead of you . . . Jenny," says Eric mockingly.

"Why?" asks Jennifer.

"'Cause we already did," says Josh.

"Surprisingly, guys can think for themselves," says Eric.

Linda bursts out laughing. She is lying on the end of the hotel bed with her head hanging upside down from the edge of the mattress.

"Oh, so you think that's funny?" asks Eric jokingly. He runs over to her and lies on top of her.

"I can't breathe, you idiot," says Linda. Linda is surprisingly strong and pushes him off of her. He falls off the bed and to the carpet. He starts laughing.

"What are you, Wonder Woman or something?" Eric begins to laugh at Linda.

"Fat-ass," Linda says jokingly.

"Anyway," Samantha says as she rolls her eyes. *My friends are weird, but I love them for that, because I know I'm just as weird as they are. Beautiful, weird people,* thinks Samantha. She continues to speak. "We got to check out before twelve noon."

"The princess's birthday is coming up," says Jennifer in a singsong voice. Jennifer is sanding her nails. She likes manicures and pedicures and loves taking care of herself.

"Whatever," says Linda, stuffing her face into her pillow. *I don't like the sudden attention.*

"Yeah, we got something planned for you," says Samantha.

That sounds like a sentence of execution thinks Linda. "That's very nice of you."

Everyone agrees that her birthday party is going to be awesome. The guys take their separate showers, and get ready for bed. Everyone falls asleep around 3:00 a.m. and wakes up at about ten. They get ready and check out of the hotel room.

Chapter Eight

We will destroy everything that is insincere.
We will evolve and radiate with light.
We shall become warriors,
But that means we can accidentally kill each other.

"Where are we going now?" asks Samantha.

"I don't know. Whatever town sounds interesting, replies Linda.

"I hope it's pretty," says Jennifer.

"I just hope it has a good social scene," says Josh.

"Yeah, that's what makes a town," adds Eric.

They are on a six-lane highway filled with traffic of different makes and models. They drive through the sea of cars while looking at the ocean. The group, after an hour and a half, decides that they will visit a city named Revere. It takes them thirty minutes to find a hotel. They unpack their stuff and sit around the hotel room, discussing their plans for the day. "Where should we go?" asks Linda.

"Why don't we just stay at the hotel?" asks Eric.

"Yeah, all this traveling is making me really tired and I want to take a nap," says Samantha.

"That's a good idea," replies Josh.

"I agree," says Jennifer.

"Okay," says Linda.

"Well, I'm staying here and going swimming. If you guys need me, I'll be at the pool," says Jennifer. She grabs her swimsuit and goes into the bathroom to change. When she comes out five minutes later, she takes a towel and heads out the door. Jennifer walks down the hall and up to the pool gate. She opens the pool gate and sees that nobody is around or in the water. The water is a nice turquoise color. The surface glistens in the sun. She checks the depth of the pool, puts her towel on one of the lounge chairs, walks back and dives into the pool from the deep end. She swims up to the surface and takes a deep breath. Jennifer is wearing a red bikini. She lets her body float on the surface of the water as she looks to the sky. It is clear and blue. It matches the pool like a perfect set. Her surroundings are quiet and peaceful. Nothing matters in the world except the pool and her. She drifts off from reality. *If only life can be as peaceful as this. If only every hour can be pure moments of pleasure. If only every day could fill us with so much happiness that it will make us implode from the inside. Why can't it be that way? Why do we have to taste the bitterness of evil? Why do we have to be a slave to the rules of our society? Why are we abandoned and beaten down if we do not follow them? I wish I really could keep a piece of a cloud. They are always so carefree and mysterious. I would give anything to control the sun.*

Splash! The sound snaps Jennifer out of her realm of fantasy in a scary fashion. She looks around. She does not see anything. She looks into the water. She sees something move and watches as it rises to the surface. The thing that comes out of the water is Eric.

"Hey, baby, did I scare you?" asks Eric in a sarcastic tone.

"That was stupid and inconsiderate," replies Jennifer.

"Don't be mad at me," says Eric playfully. He swims closer and envelops her in a big embrace from behind.

"Let me go," she says with a laugh. Eric gives her a lighthearted kiss on the cheek and lets her go. "What made you feel like swimming?"

"First, it's good weather for it, and second, there is nothing else to do," replies Eric.

"That's true," Jennifer nods. She does some backstrokes in the pool. Eric does some formal swimming, too. After a while they stop swimming. Jennifer wants to get out of the pool and do some tanning. She swims toward the shallow end, but before she can reach the stairs, something grabs hold of her leg. She looks back. It is Eric. "This again?" asks Jennifer.

"Come on, why don't you stay in the water a little bit longer?" Eric whines playfully.

"I'm just going to sunbathe. It's not like I'm leaving the pool area or you by yourself," explains Jennifer.

"Okay, as long as I still get to look at you," replies Eric as he lets go of her foot.

"You're something else," says Jennifer sarcastically.

"And that I am proud of," Eric says with a smile.

Jennifer goes over to the lounge chair where her towel is. She takes the towel, dries herself off, and lies down on the lounge to sunbathe.

Eric continues to swim. After about seven minutes, he gets out and sits on a chair next to Jennifer. He can see that Jennifer is asleep. He cannot help but look at her body. *Everything is in place. Your skin is a nice, light golden brown that glistens in the sun. You have amazing breasts and legs. Everything looks good. Your body makes me want to grab it, fuck it, and devour it.* He looks at her face. *You look so peaceful. Your face still looks beautiful even without makeup. Your lips look as if they were made to be kissed. It surprises me how beautiful you are. Why didn't I notice this before?*

Jennifer suddenly opens her eyes and stares at Eric. Eric does not realize that she is staring at him, so when he does it surprises him. "Did you sleep well?" asks Eric.

"Yes. Did you have a good swim?" asks Jennifer.

"Yes, I did." They both go back to sleep on the lounge chairs. Eric and Jennifer do not wake up for another hour.

CHAPTER NINE

Back at the room, Linda is taking a nap. Samantha and Josh are watching TV. "Hey, do you want to go for a walk and get a snack or something?" asks Josh.

"Yes, that sounds more interesting than what we're doing now," replies Samantha.

"Okay, let's go around and have a look-see," says Josh.

"What about Linda?" asks Samantha.

"Don't worry, she'll be fine here. Eric and Jennifer are at the pool if she wants company," says Josh.

"Okay then," replies Samantha. They get up, take their things and go outside. Samantha feels the nice breeze hit her face as she walks out the hotel door. They cross the hotel parking lot as they make their way toward the main boulevard. When they get there, they can see that there are many shops and places to eat. "Let's walk a little before we get that snack. I want to enjoy the day," says Samantha.

"Yeah, I know what you mean. I want to enjoy the day too," says Josh. Josh looks at the various things that are included in the scenery of life.

Samantha sneaks a glance at him. *Your attractiveness has increased over these few years. Now, I feel uncomfortable and ugly because I know I can never have you. You never show that you are attracted to me.*

Josh senses that something is wrong and asks, "Are you okay?"

The question is like a scalpel to her heart. *He thinks I am acting like a freak.* Samantha breaks out into a run. *I don't want him to see me cry. I don't want someone judging my vulnerability. Stupid relentless tears.*

"Wait, Samantha!" Josh calls out as he runs after her. Samantha did not know what was within her soul, but she runs like the wind. She can hear Josh's shouts start to dwindle away. She sees a small, grassy area with some trees and a semi-hidden bench. She sits down. *I have to control my emotions.* She tries to control her hard breathing. *Why am I acting like this? I feel idiotic.* She closes her eyes. When she opens them, Josh is standing in front of her, breathing lighter than her. He looks at her with concern, not annoyance.

"Just leave me alone," Samantha says. She is trying so hard not to drop a single tear. He sits next to her and hugs her.

"Whatever it is, just tell me. You know I'm your friend, and I'll help you with anything," says Josh.

Just a friend? Am I that ugly? Is that all I will ever be to you? Samantha thinks. "It's just that I feel so lonely right now," she says hesitantly.

"Well, I'm here," says Josh.

"Yeah," says Samantha. *And looking at you puts daggers in me,* thinks Samantha. Josh stares off into the distance as his arm that is over her shoulders begins to caress her arm. It's as if his fingertips are trying to explore something new.

"Josh, do you care about me?" asks Samantha.

"Of course. I want you to be happy," says Josh.

"I like you," Samantha says, laughing.

"I like you too," replies Josh.

"Thanks for understanding my overreaction," says Samantha.

"You know, we're human. Sometimes we bottle our emotions way too much. Then one day it bursts in order to relieve the pressure. It's a good thing that you're letting off steam. I just want you to know that if you have any other problems you can talk to me," says Josh. His gaze is understanding and compassionate.

Samantha looks at Josh as he stares out at the streets. She knew that there are just some people who remain friends. *This is a brutish moment of infatuation.* Samantha accepts this fact and moves on. *There is someone out there for me, but he is lost in a crowd of repulsive people,* thinks Samantha. Samantha knows the reason why she feels so rotten. It has nothing to do with relationships or Josh. It is an unidentified demon within her that later on in life will come to confront her. Hopefully, she will have the courage and strength to slay it. Josh holds her hand. They walk back to the hotel.

Chapter Ten

Linda opens her eyes in the dimly lit room. *What a good nap.* She looks around. There is no one there. *Maybe they are at the pool or outside.* Linda walks over to the hotel love seat and sits down to watch television. After about five minutes of channel surfing, she hears the doorknob rattle and sees the door open. It is Jennifer and Eric who have come back from the pool. "Hi, you guys," greets Linda.

"Were you watching TV?" asks Jennifer.

"I took a nap and then five minutes ago decided to watch TV, but I couldn't find anything good on," says Linda.

"The pool is really nice; you should try it," says Eric.

"Really? Hmm, yeah, maybe I should," says Linda.

"There is no rush, whenever you want to," says Eric.

"Is the water nice?" asks Linda.

"The temperature is perfect for this kind of weather," replies Jennifer.

"Where's Samantha? I want to ask her if she wants to go too," asks Linda.

"Where's Josh, for that matter?" asks Eric.

"Maybe they went outside for a walk," says Jennifer.

"Probably," says Linda. They hear the door shut. They all look behind them. It is Josh and Samantha.

"Speak of the devil," says Eric. Josh and Samantha have just finished a medium-size bag of potato chips.

"How was your walk? Linda asks.

"Great," Samantha says.

"Sammy, do you want to go swimming with me?" asks Linda.

"Sounds good," replies Samantha.

"What about you?" asks Linda, looking in Josh's direction.

"Maybe some other time. I'm kinda tired," replies Josh.

"Okay," says Linda.

"Is the water cold?" asks Samantha.

"No, it's perfect," says Jennifer.

"Great," Samantha replies. Linda and Samantha get their swimsuits, change, and go out the door toward the pool.

Josh sits in the hotel with Eric and Jennifer and watches TV. He is feeling kind of bored. He thinks about the incident with Samantha. *I didn't know Samantha felt that way. I should go see what they're up to.* He feels the need for Linda and Samantha's company.

"Where are you going now?" asks Jennifer.

"I'm going to the pool," says Josh.

"Okay," replies Jennifer.

Josh goes to the bathroom to change. He grabs a towel and goes out the door. When he walks over to the pool gate, he sees that Samantha and Linda are laughing and splashing each other with water. *I feel like a third wheel,* Josh thinks, but he walks in anyway. The girls see him come in.

"So, you decided to arrive," says Linda. Her arms are resting on the edge of the pool.

"Are you going to swim or not?" shouts Samantha.

Josh runs toward the deep end of the pool and does a cannonball. The only sound is the splash, and water is spraying everywhere. Josh resurfaces. "We didn't mean transplant the water from the pool onto the concrete," says Linda.

"I'm sorry," Josh says as he laughs.

"The water's nice, isn't it?" asks Samantha.

"Yeah, it is," replies Josh. They spend another hour swimming and enjoying the pool.

"I'm tired," replies Samantha.

"Already?" asks Linda.

"Yeah, I think I'm going to go back, take a shower, and change. Don't worry about me; if you still want to swim, you have Josh for company," replies Samantha.

"Do you still feel like swimming, Josh?" asks Linda.

"Yeah, I'll keep you company," replies Josh.

"Is it okay if I stay here, Samantha?" asks Linda.

"Sure, it's not a problem," says Samantha reassuringly.

"Okay," says Linda. Samantha gets out the pool, grabs her towel, smiles, and waves goodbye as she goes back to the hotel room.

"So what do you want to do now?" asks Josh.

"Why don't we swim a little bit more, and then catch some rays?" Linda suggests.

"That sounds good," replies Josh. After thirty minutes of swimming, they decide to relax in the lounge chairs. The sun is still shining brightly. As she sits down, Josh sits next to her and begins to massage her shoulders.

"Hmm . . . that feels good. Just what I need," Linda says.

Your skin is like stumbling upon forbidden fruit, Linda. I ache to do more to you. Josh stops and Linda rests her back on the lounge chair. "Do you think it will rain this week?" she asks.

"Maybe, I don't know. Why?" Josh asks.

"I miss the rain. It's very lovely," replies Linda.

"Yes it is," says Josh.

They both fall asleep under the sun. Linda wakes up. She looks at Josh and his body. *It draws me to want to discover and keep it for myself. I want to pull you close and feel you in an animalistic way.* Linda sighs and goes back to sleep.

Josh wakes up. It is cooler and windy now that the sun is setting. He checks to see if he is sunburned. *No, I'm fine.* He looks at Linda; her skin is not burned. *Interesting,* Josh thinks. He also notices that Linda is shivering. He covers her with his towel. "Linda, wake up," says Josh.

"Huh? What?" says Linda, sleepily.

"We've overslept," says Josh.

"I didn't burn my skin off, did I?" asks Linda as she checks her skin.

"No, you didn't. You're still as beautiful as ever," says Josh.

"I bet the others are wondering why we are taking so long to get back," says Linda.

They walk back to the hotel room and open the door. They can see why the others have not been worrying. They are all asleep. They have fallen asleep in chairs and on a mattress.

"I'm going to take a nice hot shower and relax," says Linda. She grabs some fresh new pajamas from her suitcase and goes off into the shower.

Josh watches Linda as she closes the door. *I love you so much. You are the only real and sane thing that I can hold on to in this whirlwind of a chaotic society and my mind. Nothing is real or sincere, only you; you are the only person that makes me feel free to trust. You lift the heavy weight from my soul that this oppressive, backstabbing world has given me. I wish you would be mine,* Josh thinks.

The water feels warm and soothing on Linda's skin, almost therapeutic. The sweet smell of her shampoo exhilarates her senses. *What would it be like to live in a world where every day was a piece of paradise? That place where the negative, evil, hurtful, or destructive emotions of this world do not exist. A place that will make you so blissful, it will cause you to have a brain aneurism. Where can you find places of delight? How do we create it?*

Jennifer wakes up and sees that the TV is still on. Everybody is asleep except Linda, freshly showered, who is watching TV. Jennifer can still hear the shower running. It is probably Josh, since she did not see him in the room.

"Hi, Linda did you have a good swim?" asks Jennifer.

"Yes. Did you have a good nap?" asks Linda.

"Yes, I did," says Jennifer. "You know what, Lynn? We should do something fun tomorrow."

"Yes, something really exciting because I'm starting to get a little bored," replies Linda.

"Yeah, when the others wake up, we'll all talk about it," says Jennifer.

"But for now Jen, let's just relax," says Linda. Jennifer smiles and goes back to sleep. Linda smiles and continues to watch TV.

CHAPTER ELEVEN

At 8:00 p.m. everyone wakes up from their slumber or they stop watching TV. Now, everybody wants some dinner. "What do you think we should get?" asks Samantha.

Linda looks around. *This whole scene is driving me crazy. We keep doing the same stupid things. Why is everything so boring? I need to breathe!* Linda gets up and walks out the door. She takes a deep breath of the cold night air. She hears the door open and close behind her. It is Jennifer.

"Hey, Linda, you all right?" asks Jennifer.

"Yes, it's just that the scenes of this road trip are getting boring and repetitive," replies Linda.

"Yes, I know, I'm beginning to feel the same way. It's all eating, talking, hotels, and towns with a sprinkle of random places. Listen, why don't we get some dinner tonight, and tomorrow we'll find a place to go hiking. If they don't have that, then we'll go to one of the museums they got here. Is that okay with you?" Jennifer asks.

Linda hugs her. "Thank you for always doing your best to make me feel better. You always have just the right ideas," says Linda. Her eyes are slightly watery.

Jennifer looks at Linda and says, "Everything is going to be all right. I promise that you'll have so much fun out here," says Jennifer.

"Thanks," replies Linda. They go back inside.

"Is everything all right?" asks Samantha.

"Yes, Linda just needed some fresh air," replies Jennifer.

"So where are we going to eat?" asks Eric.

"Check your phone. It'll give us a map, directions, and everything," replies Josh.

"But I don't know what kind of restaurant you guys want," replies Eric.

"Anything that is not condemned by a health inspector," says Linda.

"Right," says Eric with a smile. After ten minutes of looking on the web, he finally finds a restaurant called Marvin's. The group arrives at the restaurant. They sit down and decide what they are going to order. Eric and Josh order a steak dinner with a baked potato and vegetables on the side. Jennifer orders a grilled chicken sandwich with a side Caesar salad. Linda orders breaded shrimp with a side of soup. Samantha orders chicken-fried steak with broccoli on the side. They all have sodas or water to drink.

"This food is so good," Linda says.

"I know. I didn't know I was so hungry," says Jennifer.

"This really hits the spot," agrees Eric.

"I'm really full now," says Josh. They spent the following minutes finishing up their food. They pay cash for their meal and leave a five-dollar tip. They walk out of the restaurant.

"Why don't we walk a little? I'm really full, and I need to digest this food," says Linda.

"I feel the same way," replies Jennifer. "A walk will benefit everybody," says Eric. Samantha and Josh agree. They decide to walk down the busy boulevard. It is full of people and nightlife.

"Wow, this boulevard really is active," says Josh. They look at all the bars, clubs, food places, and shops. They see a drunk guy walking out of a bar, being supported by his friend. The drunken man throws up on the sidewalk.

"That's disgusting," says Samantha. Everyone is disgusted at this point.

"Hey, is your friend going to be all right?" asks Josh.

"Yeah, he just doesn't need any more of this," says the drunken man's friend. He takes the bottle of whisky from his friend's hand. "Here take it. It's not open. Enjoy your night," says the friend, who is semi-sober.

"Are you sure it's okay with him?" asks Josh, who can see the guy is still bent over and retching.

"I'm sure he's not going to miss it," replies the semi-sober guy.

"Okay, well, thanks, man," says Josh.

"No problem, have a good night," replies the man.

"You too," replies Josh. Josh goes back to his group.

"What was that about?" asks Samantha.

"I just offered my assistance for his friend. He says that he'll be all right, and he gave me this bottle of whisky. He didn't want his friend getting any sicker. It's not open or anything. Can any of you girls fit this in your purse?" asks Josh.

Linda and Jennifer are carrying small purses. Samantha is the only one carrying a large purse. "I'll take it then," says Samantha. She takes the whisky bottle and puts it in her purse. They continue walking for twenty minutes. After that, they decide to turn around and head back. When they get back to the car, they are tired, well digested, and ready to go to sleep. When they arrive back at the hotel, Samantha puts the whisky bottle on the table. Everybody sits down. Samantha gets some plastic hotel cups and sets them close to the bottle. She opens the bottle and pours a little into the cups. "If you guys want some, it's right here," says Samantha. Everyone acknowledges this and gets a cup. They watch TV as they drink.

"This is a good brand. Nice and strong," says Linda.

"Not that watered-down-type shit," replies Eric.

"Why don't we hike tomorrow or go to a museum?" asks Jennifer.

"That sounds fantastic," says Samantha.

"They both sound good," replies Eric.

"Hiking sounds like a great idea if there is a place to go around here. We should check a city map. There might be one on the outskirts of the city," says Josh. He takes out his phone and goes online for a virtual map of the city. After twenty minutes of looking at the map, he finds a small recreational park. It is near some mountains and has a lot of trails. "Okay, I found it. The place is called Alay. What luck, it's actually on the outer boundaries of the city as I thought. I'm going to turn my phone into a guide to get there," says Josh.

"I can't believe you found something. Okay, is it agreed that we'll all go there tomorrow?" asks Linda.

Everyone agrees and goes back to watching TV, talking, and drinking again. At about 11:00 p.m. they decide to go to bed because tomorrow is going to be a big day. No one went to bed drunk.

CHAPTER TWELVE

I want my fingertips to feel every surface that is your skin. I want to feel your pores, and the soft heat that charges my brain and invigorates my senses. I want to analyze every part of your body. Inside and out. I want to travel through your veins, sleep in your lungs, slide down your intestines, and swim and die in your gastric fluids. I want to taste your bones and electrocute myself with your cerebrum. I want to feel your skin against mine. I want you to be my source.

The car is back on the road with a full tank of gas. Josh is using his phone as a guide. Everyone dresses up for a day's worth of hiking. They buy plenty of water from the store. Linda pulls into the recreation area's parking lot. They all get out and look at the big map of trails that is in front of them, but a little far off. They all get in front of the map. "What trail should we go on first?" asks Linda.

"Why don't we go on Snakehead Trail?" asks Jennifer. "It says here that it goes by a little stream and a small waterfall."

"It would probably be cooler there too," says Eric.

The weather is starting to heat up. The other trails look just as good but they did not have a waterfall. They take the path labeled Snakehead Trail. As they walk, they come across huge rocks the size of houses that cover the sides of the trail. The rocks look like they hold stories millions of years old. Every layer of their composition screams of self-representation of their world at that time. They want to be eternal. Erasing a person or event from memory is the worst punishment that can be set on anyone or anything.

"Wow! Look at all these trees. It surprises me how green they are. I thought they would be real dry, but I guess it's the stream that is keeping them alive," says Eric. As they walk away from the intimidating rocks,

Linda hears the sound of running water. She had to focus in order to hear it or the sound vanished.

"This air smells wonderful," says Samantha as they continue down the path. Their surroundings feel so naturally right. Their spirits start to soar into another realm. The mountains stand strong and confident around them. They can hear the wind, insects, birds, and other animals. The sun shines unrealities in its gaze. Nobody complains about the heat. They only drink more water. After walking for forty minutes, Linda hears the water pouring stronger and says, "Hey, you guys, I think we're closer to the waterfall. Come on." She begins to run. The others follow. Every step she takes makes the sound louder and louder. She does a precarious thing by going off the trail. It's as if she is in a trance and something is compelling her to push her way through the branches and bushes. She sees it. It's beautiful. It is a big, deep, turquoise pool. She watches the pouring strength of the waterfall. She feels the water with her hand. It is refreshingly cold. When the others arrive, they are just as shocked as she was. The water is so clear. The sun struggles to get through the trees. The rays come through in streaks. The place looks ethereal.

"Why don't we go swimming?" asks Linda.

"Do you think we can?" asks Samantha.

"Why not? Let's go," says Jennifer.

"Wow, this place is amazing," says Eric.

"Yes, I know," says Samantha.

"Yeah, come on, we have to at least swim once in this place," says Josh.

They all agree and strip down to their underwear and dive into the deep water. Underwater it is quiet. The water mutes all sound. When they resurface, they can hear the gasps for breath and then the outdoors again.

"The water is so nice," says Linda.

"I know," says Jennifer.

Linda lets herself float. The place feels so comfortable. The sun streaks lightly keep her skin warm.

"Isn't it great Josh?" Jennifer asks.

"Yes, it's amazing," Josh replies.

Greenery surrounds them. The beauty feels almost surreal. Their brains seem to want to break down for lack of comprehension. *Is gold worth more than water? Are diamonds worth more than air? What is the price of all that we can see, hear and feel? Can anything be free? Must we always sentence ourselves to the system of business?*

They spend an hour diving, splashing, and swimming in their own little paradise. The weather is perfect. The warm breeze has a light floral scent. Linda gets out of the water and puts her clothes back on; so do the others.

"I almost don't want to leave this place," says Jennifer.

"Yeah, but you don't want to get lost here at night. You can die of hypothermia," replies Eric.

"You're right, but it's nearly irresistible," says Jennifer.

They get their stuff and head back to the trail. The weather cools down because it is past four. They walk down the trail path, past the trees, past the leaves, until they see concrete. They walk across the parking lot and into the car. They buy some salads and water at a fast food place and eat in the car.

"I was starving," says Jennifer.

"Yeah, me too," says Linda.

"I really liked the hike," says Samantha.

"Yeah, that was a good hike," agrees Josh.

"It was just what we needed," adds Eric.

They finish their food and go back to the hotel. Eric went to the front desk to pay for another night. Everyone is tired. They shower, change, and go to bed. Nobody talked much.

CHAPTER THIRTEEN

You're human, therefore
I can't trust you or myself.

Samantha wakes up. She can hear raindrops falling against the window. She gets up and goes over to the window. It is raining heavily. The streets are soaked and the clouds are dark gray. The wind blows. The atmosphere has changed. Samantha suddenly notices that Linda is also looking out the window.

"How strange. I wasn't even expecting it to rain," says Linda.

"Yeah, we should have watched the weather report," replies Samantha.

"Do you want some hot chocolate? I'm thinking about going down to the lobby and getting some for everybody," says Linda.

"Yeah that sounds really good. Thanks for being so thoughtful," says Samantha.

"It's nothing," replies Linda.

In this world, nice people are becoming nonexistent, Samantha thinks. *What has become of our human race? How did we get to such a high level of destroying ourselves? If there were more good people, life would be less painful.* Samantha looks out the window again. She loves the rain.

Linda asks the others, who are awake, if they want hot chocolate. They agree. They, too, are surprised by the rain. It is the best excuse to sleep in and not give a damn fuck about any problem or punch of tension the outside world could throw at you. This is warmth, comfort, and silence.

Linda walks down into the lobby. She finds the cocoa machine. She puts marshmallows with a sprinkle of cinnamon in all the cups of hot chocolate. She takes the steaming cups and goes back up to the hotel room. Everyone is happy when she arrives; they really want that cocoa. They all thank her and take their cups.

Linda sits down by the window and begins reading a fashion magazine. The hot liquid warms her insides and she drifts off. *What will it feel like when the world explodes? What do snails taste like? What would happen if there was no gravity? I wish unicorns were real so then I could buy one and keep it all to myself. However, it will probably get mad at me and gore me with its horn. I would then bleed to death and die.* Linda takes a deep breath. *Do you ever get the feeling that you cannot be happy in your location? I hunger for experiencing the good qualities within people, but all they give me is catastrophe, so here I am ravenous and forlorn. When I look at people, I want to cry because I see egoism in their already empty eyes. They can never give me what I need. Therefore, I feel so alone. I feel as if nobody in the world has the capacity to feel real love for others anymore. There always has to be a catch or reason. There always has to be a process. There always has to be a competition to get someone to love you. Even if you win, your prize does not seem satisfied with having you around. I just want someone to appreciate me, to love my personality. To say, "Hey, I love your intellect." Why is it difficult for people to be naturally respectful? People never love you when you want them to. Why does being alive become more complicated as we get older? It seems as though every pure thing becomes infested with disease when the populace are involved. It would be pleasant if someone were to fall in love with me now. Maybe that one person could put a stop to my detrimental ways.* Linda looks at the different clothing designs.

Samantha stirs her cocoa as she watches television. As she stirs, she feels something tugging at her insides. *Asphyxiation. This is how I feel mentally. Every day is a little more of internal death. I feel like I'm living a lie. I can walk around among a thousand motivational speakers and never really feel better. In this world there are people who will not respect you if you do not act a certain way or have money. The peer pressure of the world forces one to act like a conniving adult twenty-four hours a day. If you don't have the money, people laugh, criticize, or beat you up. Instead of helping you out or being understanding, they don't want anything to do with you. That's why people will literally die to stay or get rich. Some will go so far as to pathetically pretend to be rich. Even when they're fucking starving. I hate how dependent one's well being is on money. Everyone tries so hard to be competitive, self-confident, and tough. There are those who intend to act as gods and expect everyone to bow down to them. I want to shoot hypocritical people desperate for fame in the face. Hey, I didn't mean to frighten you, but it's just violence. You should have already been brainwashed to perceive that as normal. Nevertheless, there are days when I just break down in my room and cry. I can't go around acting as if everything around me is perfect. I cannot smile and be content with fake people and fake friends. I can't accept that as normal. I cannot accept this materialistic, perverse, misleading world as my home. Every day I go through the motions. I talk with people and see right through them. Those kinds of people don't give a shit about what you are trying to say. They are only using you for cheap entertainment. They don't want to feel lonely. To them, loneliness is vulnerability. But I disagree. At times loneliness can be beautiful. Anyway, I detest empty conversations and psycho-competitive people. You know what? Fuck all you judgmental, close-minded idiots. I'm through with all of you dictating my life. I will be me—and a big kid, too—until I die. The only thing I ever wanted was to feel real.*

Josh is tired. He starts to fall asleep. His brain fills with a kaleidoscope of colors. *Every time I see an attractive person my heart catches on a thorn. I cannot stop thinking about them. I want so badly to feel their skin and their lips. Every day when I see them, I wish a million times that something would occur to bring them close enough to me, so that they would talk to me. I wait and wait and nothing happens. They go about their own lives as if I don't even exist. I tell myself, "Nothing is going to happen unless you go up there and start a conversation." However, I cannot bring myself to go up to them and speak. Why do I have to force everybody to like me? Why do I have to devise a strategy to make myself appear attractive? If I were beautiful, everyone would beg to be my lover. I would finally get to choose who I want. Days go by and nothing happens. What really hurts is when they decide to talk with you randomly. That hurts the most because it causes your brain to say, "Hey, he or she knows I exist! There is a chance. Why else would he or she talk to me?" Your brain begins to spill out a million reasons or possibilities why the person likes you. However, deep in your bones you know it is all a lie. You know the person does not feel the same way. You tear your hair, brain, and soul apart asking yourself why you let yourself feel this way. The funny part is while all this is going on, look at the person who is making you love-crazy. That person seems happy without a care in the world. This is when the anger comes in. How can this person be happy after the way that he or she makes me feel? However, all this is erased when you come across another attractive person. It is as if they mentally delete everything you went through with the previous person that you were lusting after and thus the cycle repeats. Sometimes I want to slice my throat and just end this farce of a life.*

Jennifer is also watching TV. She begins to brush her hair. *I wish I had someone to talk and sit around with. We would spill the waterfall of thoughts that exists in our brains as we absorb each other like sponges. I want to feel the heat of someone's skin with my hands. I want someone who can provide comfortable intimacy. I want someone who I can feel. Do you want someone that you can taste? There are days when I wish I had someone alluring that I could sexually devour. However, no one is there. Life is vacant and repetitive. People are empty and rhetorical. I am full and original. Where does one belong when nobody wants them? What does one do when he or she finds out that nobody around them will ever understand them nor provide the things they need to survive psychologically, spiritually, and physically? How can you love someone who is dead inside? How can you love a person whose heart and mind is a toxic waste dump? I feel as if I am on an endless journey to find my people. I want the ones who think and have similar ideals like me. If I ever find my people, the state of happiness and inner peace and the heavy weight being lifted off my soul will put me in such a critical state that my heart will probably explode. I would fall to my knees and fall to the side. I would die smiling while blood pours out of my mouth and onto the floor. Man, I just don't want to assimilate with the herd.*

Eric looks at the clock. *Wind can feel so good. It goes inside you and revitalizes your organs, but do not forget the sun. When it wants to be gentle, it can light up the surface of your being and gently kick-start the molecules beneath your skin. It would be selfish not to include water. The water freezes you down to your very core. Fire, fire burns. Fire destroys. Fire equals pain. Fire, when properly tamed, equals a central heating system that the bones so openly desire. All these things can be collaborators or demolishers depending on their mood. However, what determines their mood? What determines our life span? Do you have a guide ready for your journey though death? Lost, lost seems like such a depressing word. Lost, lost can be positive. Maybe it will hide you from what is trying to kill you, or maybe being lost can make your life simpler by losing everything you have. What will happen if I steal the moon and the sun and keep it in my closet inside a bottomless shoebox? Will that make me a thief? How can I steal something that does not belong to any one? At least I left the stars, so that you can have some light. However, in some areas you cannot see them. Light pollution. I want to squeeze your skin and feel the underlying muscle. I want to squeeze you hard enough until I can feel your heartbeat and the blood pumping through your veins. I want to feel you past the flesh and past the physical. I want to feel something nobody has ever touched. I want to feel your abstraction, your concept. I want to feel what everyone has stupidly ignored. I want you to experience me feeling you. I want it to make you convulse in pleasure. I want you to show me your wings. I want to caress and take care of them. Those glossy wings shine in the light. They do not smell like bird, more like wild flowers. My hand touches your skin. Your skin becomes very hot. You begin to sweat. You are burning up. I try to cool you down. As I get up to get more ice, you explode in a mist of fire and ash. The impact makes me fall to the floor. The air begins to settle. I look at the dust mound on the ground. You are gone. I sit down and begin to cry. My tears drop on the floor. After a couple of minutes, I hear movement. I look at the dust pile. It begins to move slightly. I think it is my imagination. However, it moves more violently. I begin to back away, and out blasts a huge bird. It is so bright that I can barely look at it. It has the colors of the sunset. The color of fire. It flies past me, tears down my door, and gets outside. I run to the door. I cannot see it. It has disappeared. Was I ever going to see you again? How was I going to pay for this door? Not to mention the explosion scars in my house. It is a very cold, lonely night. Many years have passed since that incident. I am hopeful today because I saw something. I do not know what it is, but it is quick, shimmering, and bright. Time stops for me. I can only think about what I am seeing and later had seen. It moves quickly. It is mysterious. I do not know where it came from or why it is in my path. It is so beautiful it makes me want to cry. I want so badly to keep it for myself, to have that by my side forever. I want something that will make me ecstatic forever. I have no time to enjoy it. I have no time to converse. It moves like a shadow. It is with me and then it is gone. What hurts the most is that it is gone. I will never see it again. Why is that? I continue on my way. This divine creature of splendor leaves its trail of hypnosis. The sound of fluttering still echoes within my ears. I wonder what it was. It was you.*

"Hey, you guys. Since we can't do much today on account of the rain, what do you want to do tomorrow?" asks Linda.

"Well, we did pretty much all we could do here. Why don't we go back on the road and hit a new town?" replies Jennifer.

"Yeah, I agree. What about you guys?" asks Linda.

"I think a new town will be perfect," says Samantha.

"We'll have more new stuff to do," says Eric.

"There will be more places to visit," adds Josh.

"Okay then, tomorrow we'll hit the road, but what do you guys want to do in the meantime?" asks Linda.

"I got a pack of cards," says Samantha.

"Excellent," Jennifer says, smiling. Linda moves the table closer to the beds. Josh adds some chairs. Everybody has a seat. They all take turns deciding what card game they are going to play. They pass the hours laughing, competing, and having times of frustration from losing. But everything is okay because they have each other.

It never stops raining. It rains until the early morning. The rain clouds disintegrated under the sun's rays.

CHAPTER FOURTEEN

I nick my hands as I cut the barbed wire that separates me from you. I lift you up. I carry your shattered body out of this dark suffering hell as we slowly stagger to paradise. Je veux te voir sourire a` nouveau.
(I want to see you smile again.)

Everyone wakes up at nine o' clock. Linda wakes up with happy birthday greetings. They all change, brush their teeth and hair. They have a quick breakfast and check out of the hotel. Linda needs to stop for gas. She pulls up to a gas station a few miles down the road. "I'm going to fill up the tank," she says, getting out of the car.

"Linda, need some help with the cash?" Jennifer asks.

"No, I'm going to put it on my debit card," replies Linda.

"You sure you don't want us to help you with some money?" asks Josh.

"No, it's okay," Linda replies.

"Then I'm going into the shop to get me some snacks," says Samantha.

"I'm probably going to get hungry later on too," says Josh.

"Yes, some for the road," says Jennifer. They all get out of the car and head for the snack shop. Eric is still in the car. After Linda pays, she begins to pump gas into the car. Eric gets out and walks around the car until he is right beside Linda. He rests his back on the car.

"What's wrong?" he asks. "You look sad." He has his sunglasses on. He looks like he is posing nonchalantly for some magazine. Linda looks at him and there is silence.

She then speaks. "I'm craving sincerity. I feel drained by the propaganda of social status. I need to be around more authentic people or I am going to die." Linda's face looks completely normal except for a pair of tears rolling out of her eyes and down her face. "Everything I touch, see, feel, smell, and hear is a lie," Linda adds. She looks away, wipes her tears, and moves her head as she props up her face with her fist. She activated the switch that causes the gas to pump automatically. Her eyes mix with anger, pain, and worry.

Eric takes her hand and puts it on his heart. She can feel the beats travel through her palm. "What are you doing?" asks Linda.

"Proof that I'm real," says Eric.

"Heartbeats don't mean life. There are many living things out there that don't need a heartbeat to be deemed alive," Linda says as she looks at him.

"I love how complicated you are," says Eric as he kisses her on the forehead. *Clunk.* The gas pump warns them that their tank is full. She drops his hand. She puts the gas hose back and puts her gas cap back on. As soon as she finishes, she hears her friends come out from the snack shop. Eric climbs back into the car. When they approach, Linda sees that they bought many snacks. They are all full of smiles and happiness. It is the aftereffects of jokes and story telling.

"Hey, Linda, we got food for everyone," says Josh.

Josh always has a nice smile. It is like a blast of sunshine that makes you feel truly alive.

"Yes, and some drinks," adds Samantha.

"That's great. We don't have to starve on the road," says Linda.

They all get into the car, drive out of the gas station, and get back on Interstate 6. Eric and Samantha are in the back seat tickling each other. Josh and Jennifer are having a serious discussion about humanity's impact on the environment. Linda's eyes are on the road in a way that looks as if she is anticipating something important.

"Hey you guys, do you want to go to a museum?" asks Linda. Everybody stops what he or she is doing.

"What kind of museum?" asks Jennifer.

"There's a sign we just passed that advertised a museum filled with old artifacts dug up from around here," replies Linda.

"How far is it?" says Josh. "The sign said about twenty miles," replies Linda.

"That sounds great, maybe we can buy souvenirs," says Samantha.

"Yeah," Linda agrees, with a smile.

After thirty minutes of driving, they pull into the museum parking lot. It is a small museum that tries its best not to look run down. When they walk through the doors, a large, friendly, redheaded woman greets them.

"Hi, my name is Karmi, may I help you?" she asks.

"Yes, is the museum free or do we have to pay admission?" Linda asks.

"Oh, no, it's free, but if you'd like to make a donation, those are greatly appreciated," Karmi replies.

"Thanks," says Linda.

Karmi smiles, turns around, and shuffles off in the other direction, her hips swaying back and forth.

They begin to look around the building. It is lonely. Only a few other people are looking at the artifacts. There are many jars and broken plates behind their protective glasses. Beneath each artifact is a description of where it was unearthed, what people used them for, and how old it was.

"Hey, Jen, Sam, come over here," calls Linda in her loudest whisper.

"What is it?" asks Jennifer.

"Some old tribal clothes," says Linda.

"They're beautiful," says Samantha. The clothes are very old, ragged and in pieces, but still maintain an aura of wisdom and respect.

The guys are looking at some pottery.

"Hey, look," says Samantha. The others walk across the wooden floor to where she is. The museum has some old jewelry on display. It is made of dyed beads and animal bones.

"They must have been quite the jewelry designers of their time," says Jennifer.

"I wish I could wear that," says Linda.

"It's in remarkable condition," adds Josh. This surprises Linda because she did not know he was right behind her.

"Yeah, I wonder if they will let us borrow it?" asks Eric.

"Don't be stupid," says Samantha.

"I'm just playing around. You girls are always so serious," Eric says as he laughs at them.

"Did you girls look at the pottery? It's painted in amazing detail," says Josh.

"No, we didn't," says Linda. She walks over to the pottery section and looks at the broken pottery. The pieces are very old, but the paint used on them was very strong because you could make out the different designs. *I could just imagine what they looked like when they were brand new. The colors would have been so bright and the clay would have been strong and sturdy.*

They walk around the museum reading about the history of different tribes, special cooked foods, social life, eating utensils, and weapons of war. All of the priceless items are behind a glass case. It is incredible information. A mist of sadness hangs in the air because that age of glory ceased to exist.

When everyone had his or her fill of history, Samantha decides to go into the gift shop. She buys a mug and a T-shirt that reads *Archeology: are you digging it?* The name of the museum, Wassiah, is also included on the souvenirs. Linda buys a snow globe. Jennifer buys a postcard. The guys buy different handmade artwork created by current local tribes. They all thank Karmi and walk back out to the parking lot. Linda looks back at the museum. *Sometimes I wish I could live forever in those artifacts.* She turns and gets into the car.

"Did you guys like the museum?" asks Linda.

"I did," says Jennifer.

"Me too," says Samantha.

"That was a smart idea," says Eric.

"I enjoyed it," says Josh.

"You guys bought a lot of nice souvenirs," says Linda.

"It's something that will remind us of this wonderful trip," replies Samantha.

"Yeah, this trip is just amazing," adds Jennifer.

"I like this trip too," says Linda. She starts the car and pulls out of the parking lot. *I hope they never shut that place down,* Linda thinks.

They drive seventy more miles until they come into a town called Adawa. The name did not suit the town, because it is very modern and full of the latest shops and restaurants. It is a perfect place to hang out. They check into the Star View Hotel. Money is beginning to run low, but there is enough for the whole trip.

Everyone unpacks in the hotel room and tells Linda to stay put. They want to organize everything for her. When they are ready, they will pick her up.

"Okay," Linda says. She spends her time watching TV, swimming in the pool, and working on her tan. It is about five in the evening when they come back. They greet her, but say nothing about the plans. Everyone gets ready to go out, so Linda does the same thing.

"Linda, I'll drive okay?" says Jennifer.

"Yeah, that's cool," Linda says, and hands her the keys. When they walk to the car, Linda gets into the back seat.

Samantha says giddily, "I am going to put this blindfold on you." It is actually a silk scarf.

"You guys are not going to murder me or anything?" asks Linda amusedly.

"Of course not. Don't get paranoid," says Jennifer, laughing.

Twenty minutes later, the car stops. They escort her out of the car and to their destination. *I feel very stupid with this blindfold on.* She hears voices and smells food. *Great, people probably think I am a freak with this on.* Some people actually do look over when they see a bunch of kids walking into the restaurant with a blindfolded girl. However, they do not know what is going on. Human beings are curious little creatures.

"Okay, on three we're going to remove the blindfold," says Eric.

"One, two, three, Happy Birthday!" shout all of Linda's friends. Linda's eyes adjust to the light. What she sees in front of her almost makes her cry from being so thankful. There is a beautiful table decorated in a way that is fit for a queen. The silverware sparkles. There is a beautiful high-end designed cake with *Happy Birthday, Linda* on it. There are vases full of gorgeous flowers. There are all kinds of appetizers and main courses. Everything looks and is expensive. It is a first-class restaurant, it's all-formal. Everyone is well dressed. Linda is glad she really dressed up. *I mean, it is my birthday.*

"How did you people pay for this?" Linda asks.

"Don't worry, we all have bank accounts," replies Samantha.

"Thank you so much," says Linda. She begins to tear up.

"Don't cry," says Josh.

"I'm just so grateful to have friends like you," replies Linda.

"Aww," say all her friends. They give her a big group hug. They sit down and begin to eat and converse. Linda is having such a great time. Everyone is laughing and in a great mood. She is finally eighteen. All of her friends were already eighteen before the road trip even started. Her birthday is the last one to be celebrated out of all of them. Everybody is having a wonderful time in the restaurant and is now stuffed. Linda's friends pay the bill. Josh leaves a twenty-dollar tip, and they all walk back to the car. Josh is in the passenger seat. He turns his head back and says, "Hey, Linda, this is not all of it. We got a reservation at a club."

"How did you guys arrange all this?" asks Linda.

"We have our ways," replies Jennifer. Linda does not care to ask how.

They arrive at a club called Saint Peters. The name of the club contradicted the scene. Jennifer walks up to the bouncer and tells him about the reservation. The bouncer is a giant man with a shaved head. He checks his list and lets them in. The club is so alive. The music is pumping. There are blinding, different-colored lights. Nothing feels real. Linda feels strangely at peace. Everyone immediately starts dancing. After hours of dancing, they decide to rest and sit down. It is a great way to digest the food that they had just eaten.

Linda can see that Eric and Jennifer are talking and flirting with each other. Samantha looks uncomfortable sitting next to them. *I guess she does not like that they are flirting.* Linda sits down next to Samantha. "Hi, buddy," says Linda. Linda hates it when people feel out of place. "You wanna get something to drink?"

"Yeah," says Samantha. You can tell that Samantha does not want to be next to Jennifer's flirt fest. Josh is in oblivion taking a nap. When Samantha and Linda get their drinks, Linda sees that Samantha looks sad. She knows why, but still asks.

"What's wrong, Sammy?" asks Linda.

"Well . . ." says Samantha. She is somewhat hesitant. "I kind of have a crush on Eric." She seems somewhat ashamed to say it.

"Does he know about it?" asks Linda.

"He doesn't have a clue. What's the point in telling him? It seems he's interested in Jen. She is very beautiful," says Samantha.

Linda looks at Samantha. "Don't forget that you're beautiful too. Any guy would love to go out with you," says Linda.

"That's true," says Samantha. While they are talking, a guy walks up to them and asks Samantha to dance. He is a good-looking Latino. He smells wonderful too.

"Told you," says Linda.

Samantha understands. "You're right," she says, and smiles. She takes him to the dance floor. Beautiful people attract other beautiful people like magnets. But sometimes beauty is useless.

Chapter Fifteen

I want to get to know you
Because you don't even know yourself.

Five minutes later, while Linda is sipping on her drink, a really cute black guy asks her to dance. He looks like a model and is very suave. She accepts his dance proposal. There she and her friend are, dancing with strangers. Is life not like that? Dancing with strangers? A few songs later, they thank each other for the dance and walk away. Linda sits down next to Josh and wakes him up.

"Huh, what?" says Josh, all confused.

"Aren't you going to dance?" asks Linda.

Samantha comes back from the dance floor and says, "That guy is so cute and such a great dancer,"

"So was mine," says Linda.

"Someone asked you to dance too?" asks Samantha.

"Yeah about five minutes after you," replies Linda.

"Awesome," Samantha says, and smiles. Jennifer and Eric are on the dance floor.

"Linda, let's dance," says Josh.

"Sam, are you going to be okay here?" asks Linda.

"Yeah, I'm going to rest. I'm tired," replies Samantha.

"Okay," says Linda. Linda hates to ditch friends. Linda wants to make sure that Samantha knows that she cares about her. Josh and Linda hit the dance floor. Linda is having an out-of-body experience. She wishes she could experience bliss forever.

Josh watches as she dances. He feels emotions conflicting within him. *What am I feeling?* He pushes it out of his head, forgets about it, and continues to dance.

After a while, Linda decides that she is done for the night. Linda and Josh sit next to Samantha, Eric, and Jennifer. They all decide they are ready to go back to the hotel. It is 3:00 a.m. Everyone is sore from dancing but manages to get back into the car. Jennifer drives back to the hotel. The guys go right to sleep. The girls change, and take their showers before going to sleep. Everyone is so tired. They fall asleep as soon as their heads hit their pillows.

They do not wake up until 11:00 a.m. When they wake up, they have to get ready quick. They have to check out at 12:00 p.m. The day's events feel like a blur. It is a whirlwind of different parks, food, and shopping.

Linda is in a state of confusion. *Money, money controls my life. I feel like I am in a coma that I cannot wake up from. I, a person with a deep soul, want to take flight. I want to achieve the impossible. I feel trapped, cornered. I want to feel joy. My biggest fear is that I will not be able to find it. It is concealing itself from me.*

"Linda . . . Linda . . . wake up . . . Linda," calls Eric.

Once again, she rips herself from her thoughts.

"Are we going to another town?" asks Eric.

"Yeah," replies Linda.

Chapter Sixteen

I feel horny today. I feel lonely, but sometimes I feel happy. One time for a split second, I actually felt happy about my life. I was surprised that I had that emotion. I rarely ever feel that way. I felt free because I felt as though I was changing and did not have to continue on being miserable. I want someone to touch my body. I get restless sometimes. I have so much energy. I always feel out of place when I am around people. I feel obnoxious if I laugh or talk too much. I feel as though everyone around me is either excessively quiet and boring or too violent and destructive. It's as if no one wants to break character. It's as if they are trying to prove themselves to someone. Some despise showing vulnerable emotions. These people kill the energy in the room. Those people make me want to vomit, preferably on them. What a wretched human being, to be desperate for approval. Waiting for an approval that will never come. I always wanted to know how many feathers are on a bird. I feel less horny now but a little lonelier. Sexual organs stink. For real, they have a bad smell. Anyway, what are the ingredients in birdseed? I am thinking of baking cookies at 3:00 a.m. and eating them in the afternoon. I do not like hot days; I prefer cold ones. Why do we have toenails and fingernails? Why do we communicate if our conversations lead to nothing? I bought some happiness yesterday but it did not last. I did not want to buy too much because I did not want it to rot. Rotten happiness is not so good to ingest. It can be lethal. I love you. People rape, beat, and take care of that phrase. There are too many paths, too many situations, and too many emotions. I love you, I love you, I love. If I repeat it enough will it lose its value? Will you give up and believe me? Trust, do you trust me? Do I trust you? Trust is dangerous because you have to filter out the individuals. Who are your enemies? Be careful, angels on the outside but demons within. Hi, hi, hi, hi, hi, nice to meet you. I want to be on drugs for one day. Just for one day. Put aside addiction and money. I just want to be in an altered state, altered mentality. Travel, I wish I could travel through time but then I will just fuck up the future. Dinosaurs do not make good pets. Who the fuck invented the muffin? It has a weird shape. I hate you, I hate you. It feels good to say it. It makes you feel less like a slave and more like the boss. Soap, I do not like certain soap because it dries out my skin. I brushed my teeth with soap once. That was because I did not have any toothpaste. It tasted awful. Now I do not feel horny or lonely anymore, I just feel empty. I do not feel any kind of emotion. Does one have to feel an emotion twenty-four hours a day? No, that is too much work. Sleep. One time I really felt like I was falling. My body reacted as if it really was falling, then I woke up. Dreams sometimes feel too real. It gets scary because you feel as if you have to watch your back both in dreams and in the real world. You don't feel protected anywhere. Do not forget happy dreams. Everybody should love each other. However, there are so many violent perverts out there. Nobody wants to associate with a violent pervert. They pop the magic bubble and smash the rose-colored glasses. Snakes have cold skin because they are cold blooded. I like to pet them. The non-poisonous ones, of course. Snakes are beautiful. I wonder if anyone will invent a brand new language, culture, and race. Race—a touchy subject. It should not be a big deal. Nobody should be uncomfortable to speak his or her mind. We should all respect each other's opinions. However, no, we have to have an excuse to get violent. Violet, I know it is a color, but I wonder if it relates to violence. They share similar letters. Life gives people shit, but some do not know how to process it. They blame their hatred on other things. They never address what is truly bothering them. That is the problem; people hide. Anger, anger, anger, such a lovely volatile acid. What about sadness? Who is it related to? Is it the unwanted child of love and hate? Sadness is like a blanket, very dark and suffocating. Why do we have clouds? When did they come into existence? And why are they white? Why can't they be green? I have a picture that I drew with crayons. It lost the value it once had so long ago. I get the feeling that I have been duped. Nobody told me but that's the point.

Chapter Seventeen

Once again, they pull onto Interstate 6. This is the end of their trip. This will be the last town, and they will drive back home, which is many miles behind them. Linda thinks her poor car will stress out from driving so much. "You're a good car," says Linda and she pats the dashboard.

Jennifer looks out the car window. She is having a great time and begins to reflect. *Life is beautiful, something that you can absorb. Life can be ugly. Life either destroys or creates you. I like Eric, he is cute and flirtatious, but it's nothing serious. I have so many ideas and dreams. I want to be an artist and travel the world. I want to have a lover in every country. I want to learn different languages. I want to cook different kinds of foods. I want to climb different mountains. I want to explore nature. I want to find happiness. I love my friends. I want to live life to its fullest capacity, so that when I die, I will feel complete and my curiosity satisfied. I want to be at one with myself.*

The town is Mefora. Linda thinks that all the towns they have visited look the same. That is what happens when modernity confronts a town. "Okay, you guys, what hotel?" she asks.

"Let's pick a luxurious one," says Samantha.

"Only if we all pitch in money," Linda replies.

The hotel they settle for is the cream of the crop. It is called The Legacy Hotel. Linda and the others check in. They go up the elevator to their room. All this is possible through credit cards. Linda walks into the room. *It is so nice to be in an elegant hotel. Even the mattresses are comfortable.* She falls back on one of the two king-sized mattresses.

"It's a very spacious room," says Jennifer.

Everyone agrees. The room is huge. It is full of appliances, fixtures, and hotel gifts that scream decadence. The balcony has an awesome view of the city.

"Well, what are we going to do today?" asks Linda, who is starting to tire from all the nights out. She did not collapse from exhaustion because she has that youthful energy. *I'm running on adrenaline.*

"I don't know," says Eric.

"How about we have a picnic?" asks Samantha.

Linda is reading the local newspaper that the hotel surprisingly provided for free. It is on the bed. "What about a music and arts festival?" she asks.

"Where and when?" Jennifer asks.

"It started yesterday, and it's going for four days," Linda replies. She proceeds to read the address given.

"That sounds great," says Josh.

"So, does everyone want to go?" asks Linda. Everyone loves the idea. Off they go carrying food, water, and jackets. They prepare themselves for a huge festival. After asking directions, Linda finally pulls up to the parking lot of the festival. Light Streak Festival is the name. There are so many people. They pay for parking and have to search the huge but still overcrowded parking lot for a space. They finally find a spot. When they get out, the weather feels perfect; the sun is shining. Linda can see that there are many people. There are also food stands, drinks, different arts and crafts, paintings, drawings, and a huge stage that plays all genres of music. They pay their admission fee. When they get in, you can feel the free-spirited vibe. There are people dancing and walking on stilts. Everything is random and does not make sense. It is beautiful.

"Do you like it?" asks Eric.

"Yes, I love it," replies Linda. They begin to walk past different booths filled with different kinds of clothes, arts and crafts.

"Look at all this beautiful handmade jewelry," says Jennifer. One of them has different kinds of Indian beads and turquoise stones. Jennifer decides to buy it. Samantha buys some bracelets. The guys buy food. Everyone spends their time looking at all the art, buying some trinkets here and there, listening to music, eating, laughing, and enjoying all the entertainment. Hours are flying by. Day is soon about to transform into another animal . . . night. As it gets darker, the sensation of the scene will change.

Linda's mind is spinning. Everything is a whirlwind of sounds and bright lights. *I feel as if the whole world is fast-forwarding and I am stuck in normal mode. Life is rushing past and through me. I feel as if at any moment, if I let my guard down, I will lose my mind.*

"Those are really pretty glow-in-the-dark necklaces," says Samantha as she points to a booth. Her friends look over and decide to buy the glow-in-the-dark stuff.

Samantha feels like she cannot wait to move forward with her life. *I want to be really well educated. I want a great job. I want to be independent. I love my friends so much. Inside and out, I want to love and be beautiful. I want everything from life, A to Z. I love just sitting and watching the world go by. I want everything. I want to become nothing and everything all at once.* Samantha looks at Linda, who is happily overwhelmed by all the glow-in-the-dark choices. *I love how Linda is so free. I want to gain that access to another world. I love staying in her many worlds. I want to be me. I want to achieve the highest of highs without drugs and bad side effects. I want my soul to explode and have the dust bless the ground. I love the universe. Life, I take you into my arms.*

Linda sees that they have all kinds of colors, even a rainbow kind.

"So many to choose from," says Josh. Everyone buys his or her own.

"Hey, look, they have some games," says Eric.

They see all kinds of fair booth games. Maybe one of them will win a stuffed animal or something. Jennifer and Samantha want to shoot some hoops. Josh wants to shoot some fake ducks. Linda does not know what game she wants to play first. There are so many.

Eric walks up to Linda. "Linda, can I talk with you . . . in private?" asks Eric.

Linda is hesitant because of the unexpectedness of the question. "Yeah, sure," Linda says. "Stay here, guys. We'll be right back," she tells the others.

The rest of the group is preoccupied with their own interests and distractions. "Okay," some of them murmur.

Eric and Linda walk over to a bench where it is less noisy from all the games and out of sight from the group. It is evening, and the sky fills with purple, reds, and oranges.

"So, what do you want to talk about?" asks Linda. She knows it is something personal. Why else would he want to speak to her in private?

"Uh . . . I feel so stupid saying this. Oh, just forget it," Eric says in frustration. He gets up and is about to leave.

Linda grabs his arm and sits him right back down. "No, you're not leaving until you tell me what's bothering you. I don't like you feeling uncomfortable," says Linda.

"Okay . . . you're the only person I can confide in. I feel like I can trust you," Eric says as he takes a deep breath. "Do . . . you love me, Linda?" asks Eric.

"Of course I do. Unconditionally. You're my best friend. Now tell me what's bothering you," replies Linda.

Eric finally manages to tell her. "I feel so depressed . . . I feel like I am going crazy . . . nothing makes sense to me . . . I don't feel like I'm the same person anymore . . . I'm worried that I might kill myself and I don't no know why. Linda, I have everything and . . . that's probably why. People like me who have everything done for them end up having a lot of time on their hands to complain and self-loathe. If I keep my mind busy and I actively engage in a job or project . . . I would be too tired to complain. I feel so ungrateful, Linda. Why do I complain? Why do I feel suicidal? I am a healthy person. I have a wonderful life, and . . . I don't know why I feel this way. Sometimes I just want to die. I want these feelings to disappear. Please . . . help me. I . . . feel happy when I'm with you," says Eric as he intently looks into her eyes.

Linda looks away. It makes her feel uncomfortable. It feels like he is trying to see into her soul. Eric moves forward and kisses Linda's lips. Linda, overcome with surprise, pushes him away.

"Sorry, Linda, I just . . . feel so alone," says Eric. He lightly brushes his fingertip across her bottom lip.

Linda sees his distress. She hugs him. It is the kind of embrace where you want to feel and expose each other's damages. When you want to feel contact. They both yearn for love and affection. Eric breaks down in her arms and cries. "It's okay . . . I'm here for you," Linda says softly. Her eyes get watery. She had no idea that Eric felt this way. They sit there holding on to each other as if they would break into a million pieces if they let go. They are both trying to heal.

Chapter Eighteen

Lighting bolts and passion
Pain, fear, and obsession
Your scent is wonderful
I want to eat you up and carry you with me forever.

They both calm down and their faces begin to return to normal. Eric and Linda walk back to the group. All the activities are still distracting the others.

"Hey, you guys, do you want to dance?" asks Linda.

They all look up from what they are doing. "Yeah," they agree. They walk over to the stage. It is blaring out techno music. They all dance for many hours and finally call it a night.

They enjoyed the festival. They arrive at the hotel at 2:00 a.m.

"I really like this place. We should stay here for another night," says Jennifer.

"We can if we get more money," says Linda.

"I have money in my bank account," says Jennifer. Ah, the privileged life of a rich kid.

"Yeah, I really like this town, too," says Eric.

"How about we all pitch in some money from our bank accounts and we can stay another day?" asks Josh.

We still have plenty of time on the road. Our vacation time limit is not over just yet, Linda thinks. "Okay," says Linda. There lies the new plan.

Everyone sleeps well. They wake up the next morning and go out to withdraw some cash. After getting her money, Linda drives and waits in the car as each one gets their cash. Linda looks at the people walking around doing activities or errands. *Humans are beginning to bore me. There are only males and females. Always the same damn thing. I wish space creatures would integrate with human society so that I can see many different species and have a fresh variety.* Everyone finally finishes what he or she is doing.

"What do you guys want to do?" asks Linda.

"I don't know," says Samantha.

"How about we get some coffee?" says Jennifer.

"That sounds like a good idea," says Eric.

"Yeah," says Josh.

So off they go. They pull up to a place called Book's Coffee House. It is very homey and spacious. There are books and couches inside. They order their drinks and decide to sit outside on the patio. They spend two hours there laughing and talking about whatever interests them at that moment. They are having a great time. It is a beautiful, sunny day.

Linda looks at the sky and begins to daydream. *I feel like a rat. My life makes me feel like I'm a rat that has been stuck in a small area. I feel like life is the person that feeds me, gives me little rat toys, which, in reality, are materialistic possessions and relationships. Those little rat toys distract me from realizing that I am stuck in a small area and will never have the chance to explore the bigger part of life. I will live and die in that small area. That is what society makes you do. Buy a house, get married, raise a family, get a job, pay bills, and fuck each other. Process and repeat. They do not live another way, only following and repeating the same repetitive steps. I feel like everyone is a robot already preprogrammed on how to live his or her life. This angers and frightens me. I do not want to live like that. I want to live my life the way I want to live it. I want to break the status quo. I want to live my life opposite to that of my own kind. I want my life to be random, happy, and crazy. I do not want it to be boring. I want my life to be different from everyone else's. I want to keep my individuality forever. I feel the days melting into another. The places we go to are beginning to lose their meaning. All we want is just another high of entertainment.*

"What are we going to do next?" asks Josh.

"I don't know," says Samantha.

"Why don't we go out tonight?" asks Jennifer.

"That sounds like a good idea," says Linda.

When everyone finishes with their coffee, they decide to go back to the hotel and enjoy the scene at night.

Chapter Nineteen

I love secretly following you.
I love secretly watching everything you do.
You will be mine, and no one else's.

Before they go back to the hotel, they want to look around town some more. They start walking down the streets while looking and commenting on whatever catches their interest. They decide to go into a costume shop. When they walk inside, everyone scatters because there are so many different things to try on.

"Hey Jennifer, can I talk to you outside?" asks Eric.

"What? Uh, yeah," replies Jennifer, who is surprised at his request. She was not expecting a private conversation. Eric leads her out of the costume shop. "What's wrong? What's with the secrecy and why are we outside?"

"It's just that I want to talk with you and I don't want the others to overhear our conversation," says Eric.

"Okay, well why don't we take a short walk?" asks Jennifer. They start walking slowly and casually away from the costume shop.

Eric begins to talk. "Do you like the trip?"

"I think it's awesome, amazing, and something I need to relieve the stress, but that's not what you really want to tell me, is it?" asks Jennifer.

"No, I'm just going to tell you straight out that . . . I want to be your boyfriend," says Eric.

"Uh . . . wow . . . thanks," replies Jennifer, who's in shock.

"I just wanted to let you know," says Eric sheepishly.

"I would like to be your girlfriend, but can we start our relationship after the trip? There are just too many things going on right know," says Jennifer.

"That's fine, that way we won't shock the others with the sudden news," says Eric.

"Exactly," says Jennifer.

They walk arm and arm back to the shop. When they walk in, they see the others trying on different wigs.

"Hey, Jenny, look, I got a wig for you," says Samantha. It is a jumbo rainbow-colored wig.

"Oooh . . . let me try it on," replies Jennifer.

The others are posing and trying on different costume accessories that look ridiculous. Even Eric tries some on. After a while, the group gets tired with the costume thing. They thank the employees and leave.

"Why don't we go to that little park over there?" asks Linda, as she points down the street. It is not that far, just a short walk from their point of view.

"Yeah, that sounds like a good idea," says Jennifer. The others agree.

When they arrive, they decide to sit on one of the large benches close to the park's water fountain.

"It's really nice here," says Eric.

"The water fountain looks cool," says Josh.

"It's a nice day. I'm surprised that our trip is not filled with a lot of bad weather," says Samantha.

"That is so true, maybe it's fate," says Linda.

"Yeah, maybe," agrees Josh.

"So, what are you guys going to do when you go to college? Are we still going to see each other, or are we going to move on and forget about everyone?" asks Samantha.

"I hope not. If we do, I'll hunt you guys down and kill each one of you myself," Linda threatens with a laugh.

"Listen, we should agree that we won't let that happen and that we'll stick together as long as we can," says Jennifer.

"Yeah, what good will that do? When life wants to separate something, it knows how to make it fast and permanent," replies Josh.

"Don't be so negative. Don't you see that we're trying to fix a future issue?" says Samantha.

"Yeah, you're right. Let's go ahead with it," says Josh.

"Is it agreed upon or not? Are we going to keep in contact no matter what life throws at us?" asks Linda. They all agree that they will give their best effort to stay together. They spend an hour or so discussing their wants, desires, goals, and dreams. Everyone seems very eager to drink the world. The trees sway in the light breeze. The park is alive with human contact and the collective noises of wildlife.

CHAPTER TWENTY

When they arrive back at the hotel, they all just sit around. They watch TV and talk until 6:00 p.m.

"Where do you guys want to go tonight?" asks Jennifer.

"I don't know. How about watching a movie?" asks Samantha.

"No, I want to go to a club," says Jennifer.

"No, why don't we go bowling?" asks Eric.

"What about you, Linda?" asks Jennifer.

"No, I'm too tired," says Linda.

The others did not know that all the traveling and driving is draining her. They did not even bother to ask Josh because he is fast asleep on the bed. After many minutes of arguing, indecisiveness, and frustration about where they are going to go, they finally come up with a solution. They calmly decide to go their separate ways and do what they want. They look up the addresses of where they are going. All they have to do is insert the address of where they are going and their phones turn into guides. Linda did not even bother to ask them where. She dozes off in the chair.

After an hour or so, Linda wakes up. Josh is already up watching TV. "Where is everybody?" he asks.

"They went out their separate ways because they couldn't agree on a single place to go," says Linda.

"Where did they go?" asks Josh.

"I didn't get to ask them. Don't worry, they have their cells with them if we need to call them," says Linda.

"Okay," says Josh. Linda and Josh watch a program about people getting into strange accidents. After the program, Josh gets up from his chair to get some water. Linda is still watching TV. After he finishes his drink, he sits next to Linda on the edge of the bed. "Did you have fun on this trip?" he asks.

"Yes," replies Linda.

"What are you going to do when you get home?" asks Josh.

"Maybe sleep for a week," Linda suggests, laughing.

"Yeah, this is a nice trip. I really loved all the places we went to," says Josh.

"This is great for the soul," says Linda.

"That's true, I guess this trip has given me some sort of new perspective," says Josh.

"That's so cliché," says Linda. They both laugh. Josh looks at Linda. An uncomfortable silence hangs in the air. His hand touches hers. Linda quickly removes her hand. She stands up, walks across the room, and sits down in another chair and watches TV.

"Sorry if I made you feel uncomfortable . . . I just want to know what you're feeling," says Josh. Linda does not respond. "Linda, can you please tell me what's going on? Why are you acting so strange with me? I feel like you hate me all of a sudden," says Josh.

"There's nothing going on. I don't know what you're talking about," says Linda.

"Please don't lie to me. I've known you long enough to know when something's wrong," says Josh.

Linda stands up from the chair. "Don't you ever think you got me figured out. You know nothing about me," says Linda, her voice rising in anger.

"I'm sorry if I've offended you, but I think I've got to tell you something," says Josh.

"What?" says Linda in a tired and annoyed tone.

"I think I have feelings for you . . . I want to be with you," says Josh.

"Are you high? You don't even know what you're talking about. So this is the reason why you've been acting weird," says Linda, her anger increasing.

"Linda, don't hate me. I just want to know if you feel the same way," says Josh, desperate for an answer.

"Can you please just drop it?" says Linda as she walks across the room. She does not even want to be near him.

Josh can't take it anymore. "Linda, just give me a fucking answer!" he yells.

"Shut the fuck up!" Linda screams as she picks up a vase that is on the table, and throws it at him. He dodges it, and it smashes into a million fragments on the wall just to the side of a painting. She does not even think that someone could call the cops because of the loud arguing. "I hate you! I hate how you make me feel! Can't you see that I want you, too? You don't understand! These raw emotions are making me sick!" Linda screams. Linda's face is furious, on the brink of tears.

Josh is speechless. "I . . . didn't know," he replies. He moves closer to her and she embraces him.

Linda whispers, "I don't want to have these feelings, but I just do. I don't know how to get rid of them."

He stops and looks into her eyes. They begin to kiss passionately and fall onto the hotel bed. Josh begins to remove his coat and his shirt. He kisses her neck. His hands feel the sides of her stomach. Her lips are soft against his mouth. Josh is in a trance. She smells so good and feels so right; he thinks he feels a dose of pure happiness. "I love you, Linda, says Josh.

Linda meets his gaze. "Get the fuck away from me!" she screams. *This whole situation is sick and screwed up. I do not want to hurt him emotionally, and I do not want to destroy a friendship.* Linda pushes him off, runs out of the hotel room, and slams the door.

Josh sits on the corner of the bed. He sighs as he buries his hands into his face. "Nothing makes sense."

Linda runs through the parking lot. Her face is drenched in tears. *I have to get out of here.* Linda goes into a burger place to use the restroom. She tries to hide her frenzied face as she enters the women's restroom. She looks around. The bathroom has four stalls. The dividers and doors are black. The ceiling is a smooth white. She sees the checkered floor. The mirror catches her gaze. Her eyes are red. Her face is puffy. Linda does not like the way she looks. For a minute she is scared. Scared of herself and what she can become . . . an uncontrollable, hateful monster. *I am losing control of myself.* She turns on the faucet and splashes cold water on her face to calm down. She is glad that nobody came in the bathroom because questions would arise. *I hate when people do that, asking questions at the most inconvenient time. It is like putting salt on a wound.* Linda takes out her cell and calls Jennifer.

"Hello?" says Jennifer.

"Where are you?" asks Linda. She tries her best to sound calm and not choked up.

"I am at this club," Jennifer replies. "Can I join you?" asks Linda.

"Of course," says Jennifer.

Linda finds a pen and a receipt in her pocket. She takes down the address on the back of it. She walks out of the fast-food restaurant and asks an old woman for directions. She learns the club is not far from where she is. It is 10:30 p.m. Linda is hurting emotionally and needs Jennifer for comfort. She decides to go back to the parking lot of the hotel to get her car out. She has to do it in stealth mode, because she does not want Josh to come out and see her. It will just rip her heart out. *I hate feeling overdramatic over stupid relationships when there are bigger things in this world to worry about. Not to be cliché, but life is short. I hate love. It can be the best drug in the world. An addictive drug that can turn into a poison. It can kill you. It can make you so obsessive that it can lead to murder. I am talking about twisted, tainted love. Humans are famous for screwing up the simplest things. Only good people that are beautiful on the inside should love. It will save the world a lot of pain.*

Linda quickly gets into her car and drives out of there. After thirty minutes of driving, she arrives at the club. The place is called Divan. You can hear the bass coming out of the walls. It is a big place. *I hope I am dressed up good enough to get in.* She calls Jennifer to meet her at the front door. Jennifer arrives beside the huge bouncer and whispers into his ear. Linda looks at the bouncer.

"Can I come in?" Linda asks. The bouncer looks at her with his big cow eyes. He looks at her clothes.

"Okay, you can come in, but quickly," he says. Linda's clothes are passable and she is very beautiful.

The club is loud. There are many different flashing lights. *The smell of alcohol and sin are overpowering.*

"Come on, let's dance," says Jennifer.

"Okay," replies Linda as she awakes from her thoughts. Linda dances and really gets into the music. It caresses her soul and travels through her veins. The music and her soul are having sex or some form of high intimacy that releases all emotions and inner self. *If you lock something away for a long time, it will eventually break out. You start to forget that you are human. Your spirit and the music become one. It feels like you're evolving into something beautiful. The beats go through your head. It feels like a blanket. You feel as if you are on some substance that takes you to a higher place of being, a place where you experience inner peace and happiness. Hard achievements in the human experience.*

After two hours of nonstop dancing, they go over to the lounge side of the club. They sit on a modern red sofa and discuss life. Linda does not feel like talking about what happened with Josh because it would not help.

I don't give a shit if Josh tells his guy friends what happened. While they are talking, the issue slips out.

"Wait, what happened?" Jennifer asks.

"I yelled at him because I said that I loved him," Linda admits.

"You love Josh?" asks Jennifer, surprised.

"It's just an infatuation that will pass," says Linda. "Does Josh love you?" Jennifer asks, looking intently at Linda. *Linda looks sad; maybe I can fix her problems and make her feel happy again.*

Linda looks at Jennifer. "That's what he said, but that doesn't mean it is true. True love is when it's given unconditionally. I think we're both screwed up in the head. Maybe all we want is a one-night stand so that we can throw each other away like garbage the next day in order to fill our egos."

"Wow, I didn't know you felt that way. Why don't you just forget about him and move on? Love shouldn't make you feel that way," replies Jennifer.

"Yeah, I think I'm going to do that. It's best for the both of us," Linda replies.

Meanwhile, back at the hotel Josh tries to understand what happened. He thinks about his intentions. *I realize that I'm human and that my feelings can be unpredictable. I don't want to put Linda through that.* Josh is known to be somewhat of a womanizer. *I know what lust is, but not love. When I am around her, I feel different. It makes me feel uncomfortable because I don't know if it is love. I want her. I don't know if this is the love of the hunt and catching the prey or if I want her to be by my side through the good and the bad. This relationship will not be the typical norm. She is a free spirit with her whole life in front of her. She is unique, unlike the narcissistic, empty girls whose only life goal is to look more beautiful than the next girl. Their conversations are so selfish and idiotic. All I got out of those girls was meaningless sex. I love listening to Linda, learning random facts from her about the planet, and all her discussions about her concern for our future as a human species. What can you say? She is a nature lover. She cares about animals and yes, even bugs. She is very smart and knows when someone is trying to run games around her. She's no fool. Maybe that's what she felt tonight, because I don't know if my emotions are sincere either. She is like a breath of fresh air, but at the same time she can turn into a hurricane. She creates a crazy, pure love in me that attracts me like a moth to a flame. Sex with her would be like fire, but I'm in danger of getting burned.*

CHAPTER TWENTY-ONE

I want you to dissolve, but I am scared that I might
inhale you and you will scar my organs forever.
You are my repulsion. Just like two identical magnets.

"Well, I have something to admit too," says Jennifer hesitantly.

"What?" asks Linda in a tired tone. She is ready for anything.

"Well, Eric asked me out," says Jennifer.

"Wow, did you say yes?" Linda asks. Linda thought Jennifer's confession was going to be unsettling, such as admitting love for Josh too, but she was wrong. Anyway, it is obvious that Eric and Jennifer like each other. They did flirt a lot.

"Yeah, I did," replies Jennifer.

"Good for you. You guys will make a cute couple," says Linda.

"Thanks, I hope this turns out to be a fun relationship instead of a dramatic one," says Jennifer.

A guy walks up to them and interrupts their conversation. He whispers in Jennifer's ear. Jennifer giggles. Linda rolls her eyes, *one of these guys.* After he finishes, Jennifer says to Linda, "I am going to dance with him, okay?" The guy is handsome, but he reeks of self-interest and idiocy.

"Okay," says Linda.

Jennifer catches Linda's look. It is a look that says, *be careful, you don't know this person.* Jennifer understands and does a quick nod.

All this tension is making Linda tired. Linda decides to take a nap and manages to fall asleep surrounded by the booming noise.

She wakes up and checks the time on her cell. It is two hours later. It is quieter in here. *Where is Jennifer?* She is worried. She calls Jennifer's cell multiple times. There is no answer. She gets up and leaves the lounge area. Linda starts asking people if they saw a girl that fit the description that she was giving. Linda is about to give up hope until she asks a cute Armenian guy. He says "Yes," because he noticed that she stood out from the other girls. He points to a hallway where he saw them go into. It was in the back of the club. It looks like it is restricted to employees. She thanks him and goes over there. She gets her pepper spray out and is ready to use the self-defense techniques she learned last summer. She is in a heightened state due to the adrenaline of expecting the unexpected.

"Jennifer?" Linda calls down the hall. None of the doors are open except for one at the end of the hallway. She sees light coming out of the slightly ajar door. Linda pushes it slowly open. It looks like the kind of room people go into to have quick sex. The furniture has animal prints. There is a fake animal rug. The lights are low and mixed with red. She looks around. Linda goes into shock as she sees a beanbag chair, Jennifer lying on it and foaming at the mouth. Linda's eyes quickly look around. She sees a needle lying on the floor next to her.

"What the fuck is that? Heroin?" Linda says in a desperate tone. The band is still on her arm. Linda sees that Jennifer's clothes are off and that she is completely naked. *That motherfucker raped her too?* Linda does not waste time. She grabs a blanket that was lying bunched up on a small couch and puts it over Jennifer's body. She runs out of the room and screams for help. "Please, someone call the ambulance and the police! Please, my friend is dying!" Linda yells.

One of the bartenders hears her cries and quickly picks up the phone and dials 911. Linda begins to cry. *He left her here to die.* A crowd of people follow her as she goes back to the room where her friend is. People are talking to each other in nervous, hushed tones. Everyone is uncomfortable and scared.

Linda quickly uses her CPR skills that she learned last summer too. She took many classes last summer because she was bored, but she is grateful to know how much she needs them now. Linda wipes the foam off Jennifer's mouth with some napkins that were on the glass table. She knows Jennifer is overdosing. *I wish the paramedics would get here faster.* Her friend is dying in her arms. She hears voices telling people to back away. She looks behind her. The paramedics are here. Her CPR was not effective. Linda steps away from the paramedics to let them do their job. They try to keep her alive. They quickly load her onto a stretcher.

The police want to keep Linda behind for questioning. She asks the paramedics what hospital they are going to. They tell her Lahana Hospital. The police tell Linda that they will help her get there. Linda does not want to leave her friend, but the cops are intent on questioning her. Linda realizes that the whole entire time tears never stop streaming down her face. She is crying nonstop. *I feel as if I am in a horrible nightmare, a sick and perverse one. How could I have let this happen to my friend? I am supposed to protect her. I feel irresponsible.*

Linda begins to repeat the events that happened to the police. She gives a full description of the last person with Jennifer. He is a white guy, about six feet, in his twenties, with brown hair and grey eyes. He has a semi-muscular build. She gives a detailed description to the cops about his face.

I felt that there was something wrong. I felt that he was shady. I could feel it in my bones, but I still let Jennifer go with him. I know that Jennifer is curious and somewhat of a thrill-seeker. Why would she let that idiot shoot her up? I didn't know that she was into taking drugs. Didn't she know that some drugs shouldn't be messed with?

The detective's name is Mark D'Angelo. He is somewhat chubby with thinning brown hair. He is in his late forties and about five-eight. He thanks her for the information and promises her that he will do his best to track this person down and throw him in jail. He offers her directions to the hospital.

Linda runs out of there like a bat out of hell. She drives on the road as if the world is ending. When she finally parks her car, she runs into the hospital. Linda hopes that Jennifer will pull through. Linda asks one of the nurses if she knows a patient named Jennifer Corali and if she is okay. The nurse asks for Linda's name. Linda gives it. "Have a seat in the waiting room. A doctor will speak with you shortly," says the fifty-year-old, short, heavy nurse in a monotone voice.

Linda cannot believe this woman. Linda does not know if her friend is dead or alive, and the nurse did not even have any level of concern in her voice. It is as if this kind of work desensitized her, as if it is not a big deal. Linda wants to shake the nurse to put some sort of compassion in her, but Linda knew that it would not solve anything, only make matters worse.

Linda controls her rage, bites her lip, and waits in the waiting room with her hands covering her face. *I can't speak or function.* Waiting for an answer from a doctor feels like waiting an eternity in hell.

After an hour, she hears someone say, "Miss?" She looks up from her misery. "Are you a friend or family member of a patient named Jennifer Corali?" says a five-foot-six Asian female. Linda can see she's a doctor and that she's very pretty.

"Yes, I'm her friend," Linda replies.

"Is your name Linda Cresswood?" the doctor asks.

"Yes," replies Linda. *Can you please tell me if Jennifer is fucking okay?*

The doctor looks intently into her eyes, takes a deep breath, and says, "I'm so sorry, but we couldn't save her. She's gone."

Linda feels like someone hit her with a ton of bricks. She collapses on the floor and begins crying uncontrollably. "This can't be happening, why? This is not fair, she was a wonderful person," Linda sobs.

The doctor crouches down, gives her a hug, and says, "Just breathe. I know this is very difficult for you. I'll have a nurse bring you some water."

The doctor sounds like she is used to telling people that their loved ones are dead. Linda wonders how doctors can deal with that and then go eat dinner with their family. It's like nothing has happened. It is like living two separate lives in one body.

After Linda cries out all her tears, the nurse gives her a cup of water. The detective she talked to at the club comes strolling through the hospital hall. Linda feels sick. *I don't want to see him again.*

D'Angelo spots her and says, "Miss Cresswood?"

"Yes," Linda replies.

"I hear your friend didn't survive. Now this case has turned into a homicide. Don't worry; I have a crew checking out the crime scene. So far, they are lifting fingerprints from the syringe, and they found some hair strands. We'll also take the DNA from the rape kit that they're doing here. We'll catch this bastard and throw his ass in jail," says D'Angelo.

"I want that guy dead. But I'll settle on his miserable life ending in jail," says Linda bitterly.

"I need her parents or a family member to identify the corpse," says D'Angelo.

Corpse. Now she is no longer Jennifer the beautiful, warm person who made you smile. No, now she is a simple corpse. The cop's choices of words are annoying her.

"I'll give you her parent's number," says Linda.

"I'll give you my number too, if you have any questions," replies D'Angelo. He puts a hand on her shoulder and says, "Don't worry, we'll catch this guy."

"Okay," replies Linda, and with that they part ways.

Linda asks the nurses what room her friend is in, before they remove her body. She walks down the maze of halls and doors until she arrives at the correct room number that the nurse gave her. She walks into the room. She sees Jennifer's lifeless body on the bed. Even in death she looks beautiful. She touches Jennifer's hair. "Why does it have to end like this?" Linda whispers. She grabs Jennifer's hand, which was beginning to cool. "Please wake up and say that it's all a joke," Linda pleads in a low voice. "I'm sorry that I let this happen to you. Please forgive me," Linda cries as she buries her face in Jennifer's shoulder. She cries on Jennifer's shoulder until there are no more tears. Linda wipes the tear residue off her face. She looks at Jennifer again. "I hope that wherever you go, it's paradise. I hope you never have to feel pain again. I hope you get to do everything you ever wanted to do," she whispers as she kisses Jennifer's forehead.

Linda walks out of the room. After Linda finishes with the hospital business, she walks back to her car, opens the door, gets in, and locks it. She stares out her front windshield. *I feel soulless.* Her hands grip the steering wheel tightly. *The hardest part will be calling Jennifer's parents on her own to deliver the bad news.* "This is my entire fault!" Linda screams out before bursting into tears again. That cup of water she drank refilled her tear reservoir.

As she begins to calm down she picks up her cell. *I feel like some sort of sick grim reaper.* She calls Jennifer's parents first. She dials Jennifer's home number. "Hello?" someone answers groggily. It is late into the night. "It's Linda," says Linda.

"Oh, hi, Linda, are you guys enjoying your trip? Why are you calling so late, is everyone all right?" Mrs. Corali asks.

"Mrs. Corali, Jennifer is dead," Linda blurts out.

"What . . . what are you saying?" Mrs. Corali asks, breaking into sobs.

"She overdosed on . . . I think heroin, and she was later raped. He convinced her to use the drugs. I'm sure about that because she would never do that on her own," Linda says as she begins to cry.

"Who is this man? What do mean overdosed and raped? What do you mean? Where are you guys?" demands Mrs. Corali.

"She was last with some guy at the club . . . I don't know his name," says Linda.

Mrs. Corali is sobbing. "Where are you guys?" she asks desperately.

"We're in a town called Mefora. On Interstate 6." Linda gives her the phone number of detective D'Angelo, and then more details on how to get to Mefora. Mrs. Corali says that they are going to be there as soon as possible.

Anna Corali hangs up the phone. She is in shock. *My daughter is dead due to an overdose? And raped?* So many questions are going through her head. She falls to the floor, *dead and raped? No, this can't be possible. What am I going to tell my husband and son? I knew the road trip was dangerous. It's a car full of teenagers. If I did not let her go, she would still be alive. I'm so stupid! I should be there to protect her, that's my job.* She begins to cry uncontrollably on the kitchen floor. She hears keys and a front door open. It is Mr. Corali, Jean. He just finished his shift from work. He sees that the living room and kitchen lights are on.

"Anna, are you there?"

Their son, Feder, lives on his own. He got his own apartment a couple of months ago.

Jean sees his wife on the floor crying. "Honey, what's wrong?" asks Mr. Corali as he runs over to his wife and holds her.

"Our daughter is . . . dead," says Mrs. Corali through her tears.

"What? Who said this? We just talked to her yesterday," Mr. Corali replies.

"Linda called me crying, saying that . . . some guy made her overdose, and raped her . . . she gave me the detective's number. She said the detective wants us to identify the body and speak to us. I can't believe what I'm saying," says Mrs. Corali.

"Oh my God, so she's . . . really dead," says Mr. Corali. They both cry in each other's arms. "Our Jenny got raped and murdered? Why is this happening to us? I swear if I get my hands on that punk, I'll castrate him and beat him to death," cries Mr. Corali, in a rage as he hits the wall with his fist.

"I know. How much I want to torture and murder that piece of shit! So that he can understand the amount of pain he has caused. We need to leave right now! I got the directions to the town . . . we need to talk with that detective. I need to see my baby!" Mrs. Corali yells. She is having trouble breathing. It is 2:30 a.m.

"Of course," says Mr. Corali. They get into their car, and head toward Interstate six.

Mrs. Corali picks up her phone and calls their son. She waits for an answer. "Hello, Fe? It's your mother . . . I have some bad news. Your sister Jennifer . . . I can't say it . . . your sister . . . is dead," sighs Mrs. Corali.

"What? How did this happen?" asks Feder in a desperate tone.

Mrs. Corali responds, "They said someone made her overdose . . ."

CHAPTER TWENTY-TWO

My heart is black. There is no love, just hate.
I want to kill you and rip you into a million pieces.
Your blood needs to quench the earth.
I want to cause a solar eclipse so that
everything can feel my rage.

Linda arrives back to the hotel after she calls her parents and the rest of her friends' parents, telling them what happened. Linda calls Samantha and Eric. She tells them what happened to Jennifer. *I feel like a broken, mentally twisted, record.*

Eric does not take it well. He thinks she is playing around. However, he finally realizes that she is serious. "I'm going to stay out all night," Eric tells Linda.

"No, Eric, please come back to the hotel. I called our parents and they want us back home first thing in the morning," pleads Linda.

"I need to be alone. If you want me to come back with a stable mind, I have to do this. There are so many emotions going through me that I need some time to process them," Eric says. He sounds in pain, on the verge of crying. "Linda, trust me. I'll see you in the morning."

Linda knows she cannot change his mind or stop him. "Please be safe, I already lost one friend and I don't want to lose another," says Linda before she hangs up. When Linda calls Samantha, Linda hears her sobs over the phone.

"Linda, they have to arrest that guy or I will never feel at peace," says Samantha.

"Eric says he's going to stay out all night and call his parents to let them know that he's okay," Linda says.

"Maybe I should join him, so at least we can watch out for each other, so we don't do something stupid," Samantha says.

"What? You too? Why is everyone breaking apart?" Linda demands. *This is a time for everyone to be unified, not running away.*

"Everyone has their own way of dealing with stuff. It's a good idea to keep him company, so I can keep him out of trouble and console him about this. The reason why he's taking this so hard is because he really liked Jennifer; he even told me that he was going to ask her out," says Samantha.

"Well, he did, and Jennifer said yes. They were just about to start a relationship. Samantha, thinking for even a second about Jennifer makes me want to cry," Linda says.

"So that means he lost a girlfriend. This is too much. I'm going to call my parents to tell them that I'm okay," Samantha says.

"Call Eric and find out where he is," Linda says.

"Linda, did you call Jennifer's parents?" Samantha asks.

"Yes. It was excruciating. There was so much pain. They will probably arrive early in the morning at the morgue by car. They have to talk to the detective. All our parents want us home by tomorrow morning. They don't want us to be one minute by ourselves. I had to convince them that we could get home on our own. They all wanted to drive down here and pick us up. It's nice to know how loving and protective our parents are," Linda says.

Samantha cries again. "This is crazy! I can't believe she died like that. Linda, I feel as if my heart has been ripped out. I feel like vomiting. I never felt so sick in my life. I miss her so much. I wish this never happened," says Samantha. It sounds as if Samantha is going to have a heart attack.

"We've got to be strong," says Linda.

"I know, but this is so hard to accept," says Samantha. "Did you talk to Josh yet?"

"No, he's not picking up his phone," says Linda.

"Do you know where he's at?" asks Samantha.

"Maybe at the hotel," replies Linda. "Sammy?"

"Yeah?"

"Please be careful."

"I will," says Samantha, and with that they say their goodbyes.

Chapter Twenty-Three

You stare at me, the guest, from across the dinner table. In this golden palace, detachment and sexual tension hang heavily in the air. In your large, violent, dark eyes lies ecstasy, but also death.

When Linda trudges up the steps, she cannot feel anything. The shock has numbed her emotions. She has the hotel key. She opens the door. She sees Josh watching TV. He turns his head to see who has walked in. He sees that Linda's eyes are red and puffy from crying. She looks a mess.

"What happened? Why were you gone for so long?" Josh asks her earnestly.

"Why didn't you answer your phone, Josh?" Linda asks before crying again.

He gets up, walks over to her, and holds her. "Please tell me what's wrong, Linda."

Linda tries to calm down enough so that she can speak. "Jennifer is dead," Linda says, looking directly into Josh's eyes.

"What? How?" demands Josh, who loses his composure and is frantic. He sits down on a chair next to a table to calm himself down.

"Some guy made her OD on heroin and then he . . . he raped her. It was horrible. I found her in a back room at a club. I talked to the cops. I was at the hospital. I talked to Jennifer's parents and everyone else." Linda rattles on. "All our parents want us to be home tomorrow morning. Eric and Samantha said they're going to stay out to calm down." She takes a deep breath and continues, "Josh . . . I didn't even get to say goodbye to her," Linda sighs.

"You went through all that by yourself? Why didn't you call us right away? We could have been there with you and her every step of the way," says Josh.

"I wasn't thinking about anyone else. All I could think about was helping Jennifer," Linda cries.

"Linda, this hurts real fucking bad. She was our friend, you know? This is fucked up! She was such a nice person. She didn't deserve to die like that. I'm going to really miss her. That fucking pervert deserves to be sodomized. Shit, I don't think I'll ever feel the same way again," Josh says as he angrily hits the table with his fist. Tears fall down his face.

Linda looks at him. "Did you know that Eric recently asked Jennifer out? They were just starting to be a couple," says Linda.

"What? Eric and Jennifer were a couple? Fuck, he must feel devastated beyond belief. We lost a friend but he lost both. A partner and a best friend," sighs Josh.

"Josh, can you hold me right now? I feel like I'm dying. I don't wanna talk anymore. I'm sorry for acting like a crazy bitch. Will you forgive me?" asks Linda.

"Linda, I was acting like a jerk, so I deserved it, and yes, of course I forgive you, but do you forgive me?" asks Josh in a meaningful tone.

"Yes, I do," says Linda.

Josh brings Linda's body toward him and holds her tightly.

I want Josh's beauty, his soul, his life, and his defects. I want to consume everything that is Josh. I want to feel his spirit and his tears. I want him to experience enlightenment.

I want him to feel intimacy in its highest forms.

I want us to feel emotions from beyond. I realize that he is mine. I want his body to be all mine. I want to achieve a state of delirium with him so that everything that seems crazy makes sense. I want to grab him and have some form of psychedelic sex. I want everything that is not logic. A million things are running through my mind.

Linda felt, yet again, unstable. They stop embracing. She takes a step back. "Just trust me, okay?" Linda says as she looks intently into his eyes.

"I do. I'll heal your wounds," says Josh.

"So will I," Linda replies.

"Your darkness is so beautiful," Josh says as he pulls her closer.

Linda buries her face on his shoulder. "Stop trying to be poetic," Linda says as she looks up. She manages to get a little laugh out. "I don't want to hurt you, Josh. I wish that we could purely love, but deep within our psyche we know how to hurt one another. It's our basic instinct. After what happened tonight, I don't want to feel any type of emotion. Josh . . . I'm tired."

"Do you want to go to sleep?" asks Josh.

"Yeah," replies Linda.

"Okay," Josh says.

Linda takes a shower, brushes her teeth, gets into her pajamas and gets ready to go to sleep. She gets underneath the covers.

Josh watches TV to keep his mind off the tragedy. It is eating him alive. He calls his parents to let them know that he is okay. They were just about to drive over there because they were worried sick and getting angry that Josh did not answer their frantic calls. Josh reassures them that he is fine and that there is no need to drive over here.

"Mom, Dad? I'll see you tomorrow. Don't worry about it. We'll drive safe on the way back. I'll see you then. Bye," Josh says as he hangs up his cell. He goes out onto the balcony. He closes the sliding door, sits on one of the chairs, and has a smoke. He stares out at the city skyline. He does this for an hour.

Josh looks over his shoulder and sees through the sliding glass door that Linda is sleeping. He is emotionally exhausted and decides to go to bed. He showers, brushes his teeth, and changes his clothes. He walks over to the other empty bed to go to sleep, but stops. He looks at Linda. She is sleeping. She looks like an angel, a gift from the heavens. She entrances him. He gets close to her and caresses her hair. He kisses her on the forehead. He can't leave her alone, not after this tragedy. He gets under the covers with her and falls asleep holding her. *She's a part of my soul. I can't lose her.*

CHAPTER TWENTY-FOUR

I want money, power, and respect.
It seems I have misplaced the word love.
Maim yaham se kaham jate ho?
(Where do I go from here?)

Linda wakes up. She looks at the clock. It is 10:00 a.m.

"Good morning, sunshine, how about some breakfast in bed?" says Josh.

"What?" Linda asks groggily. Josh brings over a tray filled with cereal, waffles, and orange juice. "Thank you so much, Josh, I really appreciate this," says Linda. She really means it.

"It's nothing. I just wanted to do something nice for you," Josh says, smiling.

"Did you get to eat?" Linda asks.

"Yeah, about an hour ago," says Josh.

"Okay," says Linda. She begins to eat. She takes the hotel remote and channel surfs. She stops at some cartoons. She finishes her breakfast while watching cartoons. Linda then goes to the bathroom to brush her teeth and change. When she comes out, she goes back to watching cartoons. *I want to feel happy today, I cried so much last night.* Today, she did not even want to think about what happened last night; neither did Josh.

While Linda is watching TV, Josh watches her. *She has so much sadness in her eyes, I want to console her, and make her feel amazing.* He sits next to her and says, "Linda, I want you to stay with me forever. Don't abandon me," Josh says.

Linda looks at him "Are you trying to make my life miserable with your problems? Anyway, Jennifer is dead and it's my entire fault," replies Linda.

"No, it's not. It was that son of a bitch," Josh says as he looks into her eyes.

"I want to kill him," says Linda as she starts to cry.

"Linda, please don't cry anymore. I want you to try to be happy today. All this stress is bad for everyone," Josh says.

Linda hugs him. "This is a nightmare," she says.

Here are two human beings faced with a tragedy and in need of comfort. They lightly kiss each other on the lips. Josh whispers into her ear, "Linda . . . I want to have sex with you . . . I want you so bad . . . just tell me you love me and if you have any scars, show me." He kisses her lips.

"Josh, enough. Sex is such a fantasy destroyer. In the end it only becomes a physical, meaningless act. It doesn't solve anything, only complicates matters far worse than it should. It gratifies the body but leaves one so emotionally unsatisfied to the point of disgust," says Linda as her eyes look past Josh and become fixated on the smoothness of the hotel walls. She looks at him. "How can I have sex when my friend just died?" Linda demands in an angry tone.

Josh sighs. "Because I'll fuck you so well that you'll never feel emotionally empty again. The pleasure will wash over you like a wave." Josh laughs softly as he kisses her neck.

Linda laughs. "Shut up. Sex and love are two completely different things. I'd rather have your soul than your body," Linda says with a smile.

Josh and Linda begin to kiss. Their tongues come in contact. Josh removes Linda's shirt. She removes his. They both take each other's pants off at the same time. Josh sees that her bra holds stunning breasts that are not too big and not too small. *I can't wait to feel them with my hands and taste the flavor of her breasts as I suck and bite on them. Look at your abs; they're flawless. So flat and smooth. Perfect to go over with my tongue. Fuck, I see your panties are holding a beautiful ass. I'm going to explore her everywhere.*

Linda sees that Josh has muscular abs and arms. *I see that your body is hairless. Just the way I like it. Everything about you is physically perfect. Your face is so attractive that it hurts to look at you. Your body feels so warm, so comfortable. You smell really good too. I want to pounce, lick, and bite you like a wild animal.*

Josh wants to taste the salt of her skin. He licks her chest and kisses her. She tastes good. Linda wants to feel his skin. Her hands caress him from his torso up to his face. She kisses his neck. Josh's hands caress her stomach, arms, face, and neck. Linda teasingly pushes him off her with her foot. "You can't get rid of me that easily," Josh says playfully. He grabs her foot and kisses her legs. He moves up to her face and lightly nibbles her ear. Linda's cell rings.

They did not get to have sex. Linda grabs her cell and answers. It's Eric. *I forgot about him and Samantha.* Linda puts on her clothes. It did not take long because her bra and panties were still on. She goes outside on the balcony to take the call.

"Linda, I don't know where I'm at. Me and Sammy got really messed up last night and woke up at some random bus stop." Eric sounds confused.

"Can you describe to me what you see and the names of the streets that you are on?" asks Linda.

"Okay," Eric says. He describes to her what he sees. Linda writes it all down on one of those notepads that the hotels give out. "Eric, please be more responsible and less stupid next time," says Linda.

"Yeah, yeah," says Eric in an annoyed tone.

Linda comes back into the hotel room. "Who was that?" asks Josh.

"Eric and Sammy," says Linda. She begins to get ready. "First, I got to find out where the hell they are. I hope they're somewhere around town," Linda says.

"Do you need help?" Josh asks. "No, I'm going to find them myself," replies Linda.

"Okay," says Josh.

Linda tries to get ready as fast as she can. *I hope Eric and Samantha will stay put and not wander around.*

Josh looks at Linda, while she is putting on some makeup in front of the mirror. He begins to get lost in thought. *I want to lick and bite you all over. I want all your passion, rage, hate, and dark. You attract me. I want to rip all your clothes off. I want to finally see your naked body and devour it.*

Linda catches his gaze though the mirror. "Don't look at me like that," Linda says in an annoyed tone.

"Like what?" Josh asks, all innocently.

"Like a piece of meat," Linda says seriously.

Josh is surprised. *How easily she can read my intentions.*

"You're such a slut, Josh," Linda says in an annoyed tone as she leaves the room.

When the door shuts behind her, Josh lies back on the bed and sighs. He knows gaining her love is going to be hard work.

Chapter Twenty-Five

Here's your injection.
You are cured.
Have a wonderful day.

While Linda is driving, she cannot help but feel like she wants to destroy everything around her. *I feel like letting my angst run amok. I want to reveal who I really am. I want to be everything. I want to lose control. I want to break down and unleash everything that I have kept inside. Unleash it out into the world. Love is stupid. Love is for the weak-minded. It's for people who are scared to be alone and who hate themselves. How pathetic. Who knows you better than yourself? Maybe they're scared that their mind will hurt them if they have no one to distract them from their inner thoughts. You cannot hide from yourself because it created your hiding place.* Linda feels like her life is falling apart. She feels useless because she can't stop it. Linda stops and asks some drivers for directions. She finally gets some decent directions and in about an hour she finds Eric and Samantha at a bus stop. They look very hung over. She pulls up next to them. When they get into the car, there is an uncomfortable silence hanging over the air. "So, how was your night?" asks Linda.

"Horrible," says Eric. Samantha looks at Eric.

"Yeah, it was," Samantha quickly agrees.

"I can't believe she's dead," says Eric as he puts his hands over his face. He lies back onto the seat.

"I don't know what this world is coming to. A place where our own friends get raped and murdered," says Linda.

"You saw the guy's face, Linda. Did you tell the police?" asks Eric.

"Of course I did. I shouldn't have let her dance with that fucking asshole!" yells Linda as she hits her steering wheel.

"Jennifer has socialized with lots of people and nothing happened," says Samantha.

"Those were lucky times," replies Eric.

"What are we going to do now?" asks Samantha.

"I don't know. I'm still trying to process this," says Linda.

"This is miserable," remarks Eric.

"I didn't get to say goodbye. Linda, what happened to Jennifer's body?" asks Samantha.

"After she died at the hospital, they sent her body to the morgue. The cops say they are going to have an autopsy done to find the exact cause of death," says Linda.

"I'm going to miss her so much. I didn't even get to love her like a girlfriend. I'm in shock. When are we going to see her face again?" asks Eric.

"At her funeral," Linda replies. Linda doesn't bother to ask them where they were last night. *I'm too tired to even care.* "Anyway, are you guys hungry?" asks Linda as she tries to stop her eyes from watering. *I want to change the subject. I don't want to have a heart attack or anything.*

"I am," says Samantha.

"Yeah, so am I," says Eric.

"I see a hamburger shop up the street. Do you want to go there?" asks Linda.

"Yeah, that's okay," says Eric.

"Fine with me," says Samantha.

Linda pulls up into the parking lot of a place called Clark's Burgers. They go inside and look at what there is to eat. Eric and Samantha decide to get cheeseburgers, fries, and cokes. "You want anything, Linda?" asks Eric.

"No," replies Linda.

"Are you sure?" asks Samantha.

"Yes, I just had breakfast," replies Linda.

They decide to sit down on the patio. There is not much conversation, only eating and staring off into space. Someone left a fashion magazine on the table. *Why is it here? Anyway, I don't feel like solving my questions,* Linda thinks. She picks it up and reads it. After thirty minutes of silence, Samantha and Eric finish eating. Eric throws his trash away.

"I'm going to buy a newspaper and make some phone calls. I'll be right back," Eric says. He gets up and leaves.

Linda does not want to question her friend's awkwardness. She accepts this behavior because their best friend has died, and people cope in different ways. Linda sees Eric walk off. Samantha scoots closer to her.

"Guess what, Linda?" Samantha says.

"What?" Linda asks.

"Eric and I had sex last night," Samantha says.

"Did you use protection?" asks Linda.

"Yes, of course," says Samantha.

Linda tries to wrap her mind around the situation. *I can't believe this. What is it about a tragedy that makes everyone want to fuck each other? This is crazy. This is disrespectful to the dead.* "Why would you have sex with someone after our friend just died?" Linda asks angrily.

"I don't know. It just happened. We were both devastated about what you told us, and I guess we were looking for some comfort," says Samantha, trying to defend herself.

"Oh, please that's a stupid excuse," Linda says.

"You act like nothing happened with you and Josh last night either. You guys were alone last night, and I've noticed that he really likes you," says Samantha angrily.

"First of all, I admit me and Josh messed around, but we didn't have sex. Josh is just confused. He doesn't know what he's really feeling," says Linda.

"I knew it," says Samantha.

"Listen, Sammy, I feel disgusted that we messed around. Our friend just died, and I don't want to be involved in a relationship right now," Linda says.

"Linda, do you know our friendship with the guys will never be the same?" says Samantha.

"Yeah, now that love, confusion, and sex are involved," says Linda as she lies back on the chair and put her hands over her eyes in annoyance. *Sex, sex, sex. I hate that word. I am sick and tired of hearing it. There is no respect in it. Morals don't exist in it either. It is an agreement between two horny animals to lose control, to ravage and violate each other's body in the most horrific, dirty, nasty ways. Much is sacrificed for a few moments of pleasure. The most pathetic thing is when people try to justify it. Not all you fuckers like to hear the truth because the truth hurts. You know what you are, and you know what you do. Don't try to sugar coat your demonic animalistic behavior. It is what it is. If you enjoy it, fine. Just know what you have become and accept the title that comes with it.*

"What makes me angry is that you knew that Jennifer and Eric liked each other. Just because she's dead doesn't mean you can just snatch him up because he's available now," Linda says.

"I would never be that cold and evil," says Samantha.

"Can we just forget these stupid guys? Our focus is to help the cops catch the piece of shit that raped and killed Jennifer," Linda says.

"You're right. That should be our priority," replies Samantha. They grab each other's hands. A signal of a strong friendship.

Ten minutes later, Eric comes back. "Are you all right?" asks Linda.

"Yeah, whatever's left of me," says Eric. He tries to smile. They get back into the car and drive back to the hotel.

Chapter Twenty-Six

As they walk though the door, Josh greets Samantha and Eric with hugs. He is glad they are safe. He too doesn't bother to ask where they were. He wants to give them their privacy. He knew they felt raw, like everyone else, due to Jennifer's death. Josh then hugs Linda. They all sit around the hotel.

"This is a disaster. Our friend Jennifer was raped and murdered. We got to help the police catch this guy," says Josh.

"Yes, of course, that's the main thing," replies Eric.

"We've got to check out of this hotel and get home. Our parents are really worried," says Linda.

"Linda's right. As soon as possible," says Samantha.

They proceed to pack up and put their stuff, including Jennifer's, in the car. Linda goes to the hotel office to check out. They are off again to Interstate 6, but this time they are going home. Josh looks at the passing scenery. Eric and Samantha are asleep in the back seat. Linda's eyes focus on the cars and the road. Her brain tries to avoid remembering the tragedy. It is a few seconds of ignorant bliss.

"What are we going to tell our parents when we get home, Linda?" asks Josh.

"I don't know. It's up to you guys to figure out how to explain it," says Linda.

"I know, but it's going to be very emotional when we get back," says Josh.

"It's going to be very difficult," says Linda.

"Yes," says Josh.

"Our parents are going to go into extreme protective mode. I just can't cope with the idea that I am never going to see Jennifer's smiling face nor hear her voice again," says Linda.

"Yeah, it's horrible to be in this situation," Josh says. He turns to see that Samantha and Eric are still sleeping. "I don't know how Eric and Sammy are handling it," says Josh.

"Are they sleeping?" asks Linda.

"Yeah," replies Josh.

After a couple hours of driving, Samantha and Eric wake up. "I have to go to the bathroom," says Eric.

"And I'm hungry," says Samantha.

"We could use a rest stop," says Josh.

"I also need to get some gas," says Linda. A few miles up ahead, they pull into a gas station. Linda gets out, pays for her gas, and fills up her tank. The others get out and walk to the fast-food place across the street. "I'll meet you guys there," Linda says. When she finishes, she gets back into the car.

CHAPTER TWENTY-SEVEN

I am going to deceive you.
I am going to take your soul and burn it forever.
I am going to torture you and laugh at your suffering.
Now tell me, was that deal really worth it?

Linda drives across the street and parks at the fast food place. It's called Gobos. She walks inside and joins the group.

Eric goes to the bathroom while the others are ordering food. As Eric enters the restroom, he does not use the urinal. He goes straight into one of the stalls. He shuts the door. He begins to have flashbacks of all the times he spent with Jennifer. He puts his hands on his head. "Shut up. Leave me alone!" he yells as he punches the side of the stall. Luckily, there is nobody in the bathroom who will be scared by this. The memories are overwhelming. Sneaky tears come out of his eyes. "Jennifer, why are you doing this to me?" he whispers. He sits on the toilet and begins to cry. *I regret having sex with Samantha. I don't even like her that way. It was a moment of weakness. I know Samantha likes me. Damn, look at how fucked up our friendship is right now. We have not even spoken to each other since that night. I would rather have sex with Jennifer, but she is dead, murdered actually.* His body fills with rage. *Why did you kill her, you stupid motherfucker? I swear if I find you, I'm going to rape you ten times worse after I break your face!* Eric then laughs hysterically. Here he is having a mental breakdown in a public restroom.

"Where's Eric?" asks Linda. She worries because she knows he is a little more unstable than the rest.

"I think I saw him go into the restroom," says Josh.

"Okay," says Linda.

"So . . . uh . . . have her parents identified her body?" asks Samantha.

The question is like an electric shock to everyone. Linda takes a deep breath and speaks. "When I called them, they said they were going to leave right then and there, so they probably were at the . . . morgue in the morning," Linda has difficulty speaking about the details of Jennifer's death.

"Okay," says Samantha.

Everyone looks sad and drained. Eric comes back from the restroom.

"What are you guys talking about?" he asks. He then catches their gazes. "Oh." He sits next to Linda. "So when do you think they're going to catch this guy?" asks Eric.

"Very soon, I hope," says Linda. Linda begins to cry. Eric hugs her and she buries her face in his chest.

"This is miserable for all of us," says Eric. Josh agrees, but he cannot help but feel jealous that Eric is comforting Linda instead of him.

Linda stops crying. "I'm going back to the car," she says as she wipes her tears.

"We'll go with you," says Samantha. They take their food and walk back to the car. "Are you sure you want to continue driving, Linda?" asks Samantha.

"Yeah, I can handle it," says Linda.

As they are driving back home, Eric falls asleep again. Samantha looks at Eric. *I know it was just a one-night stand, but I still like you.* Samantha looks at Linda. *I still have Linda. Linda, you're my anchor in this tough time. I don't know what I would do without you. I feel dizzy and sick. Like the universe and all of its contents have collapsed on me. Everything is spinning. Nothing feels real. Nothing sounds real. I feel as if I am in a parallel universe, in a nightmare. I can't believe that Jennifer is dead. I feel like I have fallen in a dark void and cannot climb out. The fear is overwhelming me.* She looks out the car window, trying to find answers in the objects that pass her by.

Everyone spends his or her time being either silent or engaging in small talk. When they arrive back in their hometown, Linda drops everyone off at their own houses. Their parents are waiting outside, scared and desperate to hold their kids out of fear that they might lose them, too. Linda drops off Jennifer's belongings and heads home. Linda parks in her driveway and walks into her house. Her parents are waiting in the living room.

"Oh my God, Linda, are you all right? I can't believe what happened," says Mrs. Cresswood, crying. She runs to her daughter, hugs her, and kisses her on the forehead.

"Linda, I'm so glad you made it home," says Mr. Cresswood as he hugs his daughter and kisses her on the head. Linda's parents look so relieved to see that their daughter is okay.

Linda hears her brother coming down the stairs. David walks up to her and gives her a big hug. "It's good to see you again," says David.

"Thanks," replies Linda.

They all sit down in the living room while Linda explains in detail about what happened to Jennifer, the police, and everything. The conversation lasts about an hour.

"I don't know what to say. This is a lot to take in. I feel so bad for her and her family. I just can't imagine the hell they're going through," says Mr. Cresswood. He then looks at his watch. "Hmm, I'm going to be late for work." He gets up and grabs everything he needs. "I wish that I could stay. Everyone just be safe. Bye," says Mr. Cresswood as he walks out the door.

"Bye, Daddy," says Linda.

"Bye, honey," says Mrs. Cresswood.

"Later, Dad," says David. David looks at the clock in the living room. "Oh, man I forgot that my shift changed." He quickly gets ready for his job as a waiter. He leaves twenty minutes after Mr. Cresswood. "Bye, I'll bring back some food, okay?" David says.

"Okay," says Linda.

"Perfect," says Mrs. Cresswood.

He gets into his car and leaves. The house is empty. Mrs. Cresswood breaks the silence. "I should have never let you go on that trip. None of this would have happened if I didn't let you go."

"Mom, I already feel bad about this," replies Linda.

"It was an irresponsible idea to let a bunch of teenagers go off on their own. I can't believe your friend Jennifer died. Why didn't you watch out for her?" asks Mrs. Cresswood.

Linda's blood boils. "I try to do my best. Don't you know that I try to be a good friend? I feel guilty that she died due to my negligence. I'm supposed to protect her and keep her safe. That's what a friend does. I hate that you never trust me. What's wrong with you? I try to make you proud; isn't that enough for you to love me?" Linda is yelling.

Mrs. Cresswood stares at her daughter sternly. "Linda, lower your voice. Don't you ever talk to me like that again. All I am saying is that the road trip was unsafe. We, the parents, should have never let a bunch of unsupervised eighteen-year-olds go on a road trip. I didn't mean to make you feel guilty about her death. I just feel that it could have been prevented."

"Mom, eighteen-year-olds are legally adults. I know we're still little, but in the eyes of the law we're considered responsible for ourselves. You can't keep kids locked away from the world. We know that it's a nightmare out there. But we can't let that stop us from living. The only thing we can do is be smart to avoid trouble and be prepared to defend ourselves if we must," says Linda.

"Yes, Linda, I know. I just want you to know that I do trust and love you very much. What happened to Jennifer is horrible. It scares me because I worry that it could happen to you . . . come here," says Mrs. Cresswood.

Linda walks over. Mrs. Cresswood holds her daughter as they rock slowly from side to side. They start crying. *I feel like I have failed to protect you, Linda. I feel like an irresponsible mother.* "I'm sorry, Linda, about everything," says Mrs. Cresswood.

"I'm sorry too, Mom . . . I'm going to go to sleep," says Linda.

"Okay," says Mrs. Cresswood.

Linda goes upstairs, takes a shower, and goes straight to sleep.

Chapter Twenty-Eight

I want to be your religion.
I want to be your God.
Because I lack confidence in myself.

Linda wakes up the next morning at 11:00 a.m. She changes and hangs around the house. It looks as though it might rain. Linda spends her day watching TV and playing video games. Around five in the afternoon, Linda hears the phone ring. She picks it up. "Hello?"

It is Detective D'Angelo. "I'm calling to say that Jennifer's body has been identified by her parents. The autopsy report came back that she died due to a heroin overdose. The drug was the pure kind. Someone must have paid big money to obtain it. We ran the fingerprints and semen samples found at the scene and from her through the system. They couldn't find a match. They didn't find any of Jennifer's prints on the syringe, only his," says D'Angelo.

I knew Jennifer would never do that to herself, but she was reckless at times, Linda thinks.

"My hypothesis about what happened is that he had the drugs and probably convinced her to try it with him. He might have injected himself first and then, being strung out, ended up giving her more than the normal dosage. She then passes out and wasn't waking up. That's when he decides to take advantage of her. When he finishes raping her and sees her foaming at the mouth, he gets scared and runs away. There aren't any signs of resistance on her body," says Detective D'Angelo.

Sharing needles and violating her like that. Disgusting. I wonder what was going through her mind when she was dying. Linda shudders.

The detective continues to talk. "That's the hypothesis I got going for this case. Once we get the sufficient evidence, we're probably going to charge him with involuntary manslaughter and rape. Based on the situation, we don't think the sex was consensual. We'll catch him. I promise you that he will do his time," says D'Angelo.

"Did you tell this to Jennifer's parents?" asks Linda.

"Yes, I just wanted to let you know we're working hard to arrest him," says D'Angelo.

"Yeah, okay," says Linda. *This whole conversation is depressing.* Linda looks out the window.

"I'll talk to you again. Get some rest. Bye," says

D' Angelo.

"Okay, bye," says Linda and hangs up the phone.

"Who was that?" asks Mrs. Cresswood, who had just come in from work. She walks into the kitchen.

"It was the detective. He said that from the evidence they got, they think that they went in that room to do heroin. The cop told me it was definitely heroin. He gave her too much. She passed out. He then raped her and freaked out and ran when he discovered she was overdosing," says Linda as she sighs. *I am tired of feeling like a reporter for death.*

"Okay, I'm glad they're making progress. Hopefully, they'll have some leads to catch that sick pervert," says Mrs. Cresswood. Mrs. Cresswood looks at her daughter. She can see the emptiness and heartache in her daughter's eyes. She walks over to her and hugs her. Linda feels like crying, but she can't. There are no more tears.

"Why don't you get some more sleep?" says Mrs. Cresswood.

Linda manages to get a little laugh out. "That's what the detective said," she says. She goes back upstairs to her room. *I feel so tired. I want to sleep forever. I want my friend back. I want everything to be uncomplicated. I want misery to stop being my friend. I want sadness to stop haunting me. I feel so confused, so angry. I want to forget my life and everything. Happiness has abandoned me for someone else.* Linda walks into her room, and closes the door. It begins to rain heavily. *Rain is beautiful.* Linda opens the window. The cold air brushes past her. "Rain, why do you have to be so dramatic?" whispers Linda. She sits on the windowsill and looks at her backyard. She climbs through the window and on to the roof. She stands up on the rooftop and lets the rain soak her. *I want to feel you, Jennifer. I want to find my inner peace. I want to breathe in the world.* She looks at the sky. *I want to absorb happiness. I want to feel again.*

She lies down and falls asleep. The rain is her blanket, her protection, and her last link to sanity. She falls asleep on the roof. She is nature's child again and she can feel her love. When Linda wakes up, she is shivering. It is nighttime. The rain has stopped. She climbs back into her bedroom. Linda looks at her clock. She was out there for a couple hours. Linda takes a hot shower. It makes her feel better. She changes into her pajamas and turns on her TV. She channel surfs just as her cell rings. She did not want to answer it. *I hate talking now.* She feels like she has to answer it though.

"Hello?" says Linda.

"Hi Linda, it's Sammy," says Samantha.

Linda smiles. "It's nice to hear your voice," says Linda.

"You too, so how you holding up?" asks Samantha.

"Barely. I just talked to the detective. He says that the drug that killed Jennifer has been identified as highly concentrated heroin. He said that Jennifer and the guy were in that room to do drugs and that she consented to being shot up with the heroin. The detective thinks the suspect was high and gave her too much of the concentrated dose and she then passed out. He then raped her. You know I agree with the detective. I don't think she would have consensual sex with a stranger so quickly. She's not that kind of girl. Anyway, later when he found out she was overdosing, he freaked out and ran. They couldn't find any signs of resistance. So that also contributes to their assumption of what happened. He's going to be charged with involuntary manslaughter and rape," says Linda.

"I agree with you too. That guy definitely raped her. I wished they caught that idiot already," replies Samantha.

"I know, they already put the DNA they obtained from the crime scene and the semen found on her through the system, but they couldn't find a match," says Linda.

"What bad luck. I'm scared that we will be part of the group of people who never get to find the murderers who killed their friends or family," says Samantha.

"I don't even want to think about that. It makes me sick. I just want to think that they're going to catch this guy," says Linda.

"I know. I just hope we're lucky enough to get some justice," replies Samantha.

"I'll talk to you later, Sammy. I feel so exhausted right now," says Linda.

"This is hard on everybody and it has really affected me. Well, have a good nap, Lynn," says Samantha.

"Sammy?" says Linda suddenly.

"Yes?" replies Samantha.

"Thank you for being a great friend and supporting me. We'll get through this," says Linda.

"Of course. You're my best friend, and I care about you," says Samantha.

"Thanks, take care, and bye, Sammy. I love you," says Linda.

"Love you too, bye," Samantha says.

Linda hangs up the phone. She gets under her bed covers and falls asleep.

Chapter Twenty-Nine

I want to break you down.
I want you to feel vulnerable.
It is the only way that you will ever truly understand me.

Linda wakes up. The sun's rays shine on her bed. She feels warm and comfortable. She hears someone knocking on her door. "Come in," Linda calls. It is her brother.

"Hey, Linda, are you all right?" asks David.

"Yeah," says Linda.

"Mom and Dad say breakfast is ready and they want you to get something to eat," says David.

"You actually sound like you're worried about me," Linda replies with a laugh.

"Hey, I know I'm your brother and that I can be a real pain in the ass sometimes, but you're my sister, and I can see that all this stuff is hurting you," replies David. He walks over and sits right beside her. "Come on, do you want to eat or not?" asks David as he gives her a light, playful shove.

Linda feels hungry. "Yeah, I do," says Linda as she gets out of bed.

David sees that she looks half-dead. *I don't like my sister looking so different from her regular self. I wish I could undo all these problems so that she can be happy. Life is very strange. We prepare so much for the future and that's the responsible way, but we tend to forget the present in the process. Our lives can end at any moment. How frail human beings are. We try so hard in life to prove we are invincible, but it's all a lie.*

David and Linda walk down the steps. Linda can smell pancakes, sausages, and eggs. It is a very inviting smell.

"Hello, honey. You feeling better?" asks Mrs. Cresswood.

"Yeah . . . thanks for asking, Mom," says Linda.

"We cooked some of your favorites," says Mr. Cresswood.

"Thanks, Dad," says Linda. Linda and David sit down at the table. The whole family begins to dig in. *The food tastes delicious,* thinks Linda. She sips some of her orange juice. After the meal, Linda feels stuffed. *I need some fresh air. I feel like walking.* "I'm going for a walk, okay?"

"Be careful," says Mr. Cresswood.

"Yes, sweetie, be careful," says Mrs. Cresswood.

"Okay," Linda replies. She closes the door behind her. The sun is shining beautifully as it always does after it rains. Linda walks around the neighborhood. She hears a car honk behind her. She turns around and sees that it is Eric. *What a small town,* she thinks.

Eric rolls down the passenger window. "What are you doing?" he asks.

"Walking," replies Linda.

"Hey, Linda, I need to talk to you. I was going to call you, but I saw you walking. Samantha . . . uh . . . told me what the detective said. Sammy also told Josh too, if you're wondering," says Eric.

"Can I get in?" asks Linda.

"Of course," replies Eric. He unlocks his car. Linda gets in. Eric has one of those new black Mustangs with vertical white stripes. He starts driving.

"This whole thing is just a trip. I feel like I am trying so hard just to function normally," says Eric.

"I know what you mean. I just can't imagine what her parents are feeling. I mean, they were the ones who lost a daughter. They had to identify her body, and talk with the police. Some of the horrible shit I had to go through that night," Linda says.

"I can't imagine how they feel. Linda, I wanted to talk with you because I don't want you to think for even a second that Jennifer's death was your fault," says Eric.

"But I do feel responsible, because I came up with this road trip, and I let her go off with that creep. If I hadn't, she would still be alive," says Linda.

"That's not true. The road trip we had was great. You probably gave her the best last moments of her life," replies Eric.

"You might be right. Maybe her death was out of my control," says Linda, sighing.

"I want to also let you know that I care a lot about you. You . . . mean a lot to me. You're an easy person to talk and listen to. I really like that in you. I just want to thank you for putting up with me," says Eric with a smile.

"You're not a burden, you're an awesome person, Eric. I should be thanking you instead for putting up with me," says Linda. They both laugh.

Eric drives back to Linda's home to drop her off. As she gets out, Eric lightly grabs hold of her hand and looks into Linda's eyes. "No one can ever see what's coming, so don't be so hard on yourself. Jennifer would never blame you for what happened."

"Yeah, you're right," replies Linda. She gets out of the car and waves goodbye as he drives off. Linda goes back into her house.

"How was your walk?" asks Mrs. Cresswood

"Fine," says Linda.

"It's nice to get some fresh air."

"Yes it is," replies Linda. Linda has a sudden urge to go swimming in her pool. She changes into her bathing suit and spends the next couple of hours just swimming in her pool.

Meanwhile, her parents are discussing the tragedy in the living room. "I hope Linda recovers from this," says Mr. Cresswood.

"Yes, I'm worried. She hasn't been herself," says Mrs. Cresswood.

"I just can't believe what happened to Jennifer. I remember when Linda would bring Jennifer over for sleepovers and birthday parties when they were younger. I just can't comprehend something like this could happen. I can't imagine the pain Jennifer's parents must feel," says Mr. Cresswood.

"I know," agrees Mrs. Cresswood. Suddenly David walks across the hall toward the stairs. "David, honey? Come here," she says.

David stops and walks toward them. "David, please be nice to your sister during this difficult time, okay?" says Mrs. Cresswood.

"I will," says David.

"You better, or we're going to have some problems," says Mr. Cresswood.

"Yeah, I know," says David.

"Okay then," says Mrs. Cresswood.

David proceeds up the stairs. The Cresswoods continue their conversation. Linda gets out of the pool and goes upstairs to take a shower. She spends the following hours watching mindless TV shows. She turns off the TV and starts reading a novel. She falls asleep with the book against her chest.

The next morning Linda wakes to the sound of her telephone ringing. "Hello?" Linda says groggily.

"It's me, Sammy. You still asleep?" Samantha asks.

"Kinda," replies Linda. Linda looks at her clock. It is 10:30 a.m.

"I was wondering if you wanted to go to the mall today?" asks Samantha.

"Yeah, that sounds great," says Linda.

"I'll pick you up at noon, okay?" says Samantha.

"Okay," Linda says. She begins to get ready. By the time twelve o' clock comes around she is ready to go out. She hears a honk outside her window. She sees Samantha in her white Mercedes-Benz. She grabs her purse and heads down the stairs. Her mom is talking business on the phone. "I'm going to the mall with Samantha, Mom," says Linda.

Mrs. Cresswood puts the phone down for a second and says, "Okay, Lynn, have fun," She resumes talking on the phone.

Linda gets into Samantha's car. "Hey, girl. You ready to go shopping?" asks Samantha.

"Yeah."

"Okay, let's go."

Fifteen minutes later, they pull into their local shopping mall's huge parking lot. They luckily find a space. When they walk through the mall doors, they instantly feel the refreshing air-conditioner.

"Look at that store. Let's go there first," says Samantha.

"That looks nice," replies Linda.

They go into a boutique called Sadie's.

"Look, isn't this a nice purse?" asks Samantha.

Linda looks at Samantha. Their friend Jennifer is dead, but here they are shopping. *Human beings desensitize death.* "That bag is beautiful. Why don't you get an outfit that goes with it?" asks Linda.

"That's a good idea," says Samantha. She begins looking around the store for the right clothes. Linda looks at some bracelets. After ten minutes or so, Samantha runs over to Linda. "Look, what about this?" She holds a graphic tee and some pants that matched the color of her purse.

"That's great," says Linda.

"Aren't you going to buy something?" asks Samantha.

"Yes," says Linda. Linda walks over and picks up a bracelet that she was looking at. She picks out a coat, shirt, and some pants. She also buys some shoes. They pay and decide to go look at some other shops.

They go into a perfume shop and sample some perfume. They each buy some. After shopping at various stores, they decide to stop and rest at the food court.

"Wow, that was a lot of shopping," says Linda.

"Yeah, my feet are killing me," replies Samantha.

"You want to get something to eat?" asks Linda.

"That sounds good," replies Samantha.

Linda ends up ordering a pizza calzone with a medium soda. Samantha buys a Philly cheese steak sandwich and a regular soda. While they eat Linda asks, "So, have you and Eric talked lately?"

Samantha looks at Linda. "Yes, we talked about the whole Jennifer issue, but our conversation was quick and awkward. It didn't feel natural. I feel as if Eric is treating me like a stranger," she says.

Linda sighs. "Some things in life don't turn out as you would expect. Just forget about it. If he comes around, great; if not, who cares?" replies Linda.

"You're right," says Samantha. "Anyway, how are things going with you and Josh?"

Linda begins to get lost in thought. *How can friends turn into lovers? How can perfection evolve into disaster?* "I don't know. I'm perplexed," replies Linda.

"I think you guys would make a cute couple. He's really attractive," says Samantha.

Linda laughs and says, "You can have him."

"Uh, no thank you. I don't need any more problems," Samantha says with a smile.

They finish their food and drinks. "You want to go look at some more shops?" asks Linda.

"Yeah, I want to look for some lingerie," says Samantha with a devious smile.

Linda laughs and says, "Whatever floats your boat."

They spend the next few hours talking, laughing, and going through a whirlwind of different shops. Linda buys a purse. Samantha buys a scarf along with other things. By the time they finish buying what they want, it is evening.

"That was entertaining," says Linda.

"It would have been more fun if Jennifer was here with us," says Samantha.

"Yes, it does feel incomplete," says Linda.

"But anyway, I've had a wonderful time with you," says Samantha.

"Thanks for the compliment," says Linda with a smile. They walk back to Samantha's car.

"I just want to let you know that you're my anchor through these tough times. Thanks for being by my side," says Samantha.

Linda looks at Samantha. "I feel the same way," she says, and she really means it.

"It's nice to hear that," says Samantha. They put all their shopping bags in the back seat. On their way back to Linda's house, they begin to tell jokes. Samantha pulls up to Linda's house and drops her off.

"Thanks for a great time. I love the clothes that we bought. It was nice hanging out with you," says Linda.

"We need to take a break from all this misery. I enjoyed your company," says Samantha.

"Love you. Don't forget to call me," says Linda.

"Okay," says Samantha.

Linda takes all her bags out of the car and walks to her house. As Linda opens her front door, she can hear Samantha's car driving away. Linda sees that nobody is home. They were off doing their own things. She walks upstairs and toward her room. Linda opens her bedroom door and drops her shopping bags next to her nightstand. She takes a shower, changes, and falls asleep. It did not matter to her that it was early. She wanted to hibernate.

Chapter Thirty

The next morning she wakes to the sound of a beep from her phone. Linda slept through the ringing, but someone left a message. She checks on it. "Hello, Linda, it's Josh. I need to talk with you in person. Meet me at Bell Park in ten minutes. I'll be waiting on a bench. See you there." *Beep* says the voice mail.

Linda looks at the clock. It is ten o' clock in the morning. The voicemail says that the call is seven minutes old. Linda knows what park he is talking about. She and the others used to hang out there when they got bored. She changes, gets ready, and leaves her house. She tells her parents that she is leaving to see a friend and that she will eat breakfast later.

Linda gets into her car and drives to Bell Park. She parks her car. She gets out and looks around trying to find Josh. She suddenly catches a glimpse of him. He is wearing jeans, Converses, and a white

T-shirt with a black, hooded, zipper jacket. He is sitting on a bench exactly as he said. She walks over to him.

"Hey," Josh says.

"Hi," says Linda. She sits down.

"Linda, I called you here because I need to talk to you. We haven't spoken to each other face-to-face for a couple of days. I want to be close to you more often. I just want to be with you."

Not this again, thinks Linda. "Josh, listen, my brain can't handle a relationship right know. The love mixed with garbage. Fuck, I wish my mind would leave my body to wander the universe. That way it won't have to endure any more pain," says Linda.

"Well . . . if your intellect does decide to wander, you might end up in a vegetative state," replies Josh.

Linda smiles half-heartedly. "I just want to talk with God or gods. I want to explore every religion and I want to be no religion. I want you. I want to see every part of you. I want to travel through you," Linda says as she looks off to the distance.

Josh looks at her and smiles. "I wish I was like you, Linda. You're something I never experienced before. Maybe that's why I'm drawn to you," says Josh. Some trees swaying in the park distract him. When he looks at Linda again, he sees that she has walked over to a flowerbed. She has a bumblebee crawling on her arm. "What are you doing? You're going to get stung," says Josh worriedly.

"So what. I prefer its company. Here. Take beautiful risks," says Linda as she hands him the bumblebee.

"No, that's okay," says Josh, taking a step back.

"Stop being a sheep, and live," says Linda.

"Okay, fine," says Josh. He lets Linda put the bumblebee on his hand. Every time the bee buzzes, the vibrations make him feel as if got stung but it's not true.

Linda laughs. "They can feel what you feel. All living things are interconnected, whether we want to believe it or not. Just breathe." She smiles at him.

Josh takes a deep breath. The small fear he has begins to wane.

"This bumblebee is fucking huge and loud," Josh comments, with a laugh. It amuses Josh as it walks across his arm like a clumsy drunk. Josh pets the bumblebee lightly on the head and puts it back on a flower. "Linda, you're making me do weird things," says Josh, laughing.

"Maybe what's weird is really normal," replies Linda with a laugh. It starts to get windy. Linda turns to face into where the wind is blowing. She closes her eyes and breathes deeply.

"What are you doing now?" asks Josh.

"Stop asking questions, because you're interrupting me. Anyway, you wouldn't understand. You'll just make fun of me if I told you," says Linda.

"I'm sorry, but tell me. I won't be mean," says Josh.

Linda laughs. "It's nothing, but sometimes when I'm among the elements, it feels as though my ancestors are trying to speak to me. You could try it, but don't expect the same results," Linda says.

Josh closes his eyes, and as the strong wind current blows past him, he breathes in deeply and concentrates. As he takes that breath, he feels a strange sensation of fear, power, love, and antiquity. He then exhales. He shudders and feels peace of mind. "I get what you mean. I'm so stupid. I never gave much thought to those before me. All their sacrifices, love, happiness, and pain. It was everything they went through that made us who we are today," says Josh.

Linda looks at Josh in a way that made him realize that she knew exactly what he was talking about. "We humans are so egocentric. We don't care who we damage as long as we get what we want. We feel no remorse. We feel no obligation to either help or treat one another with dignity and respect. I can't understand how affliction is the societal norm. Don't people know that life is not simply what you can taste, touch, and feel? That's only a small part of it. Another life exists out there. It's unexplainable. It rules by emotions, abstract thoughts, and nature. It is there, where our society, civilization, and materialism are dead. Curse my self-awareness, but all I can do is share with others. Hopefully they can get some useful advice from my disorientation. It . . . just hurts to see people live a fake life. They are completely oblivious. They don't even know that they are wallowing in their own shit. Most of them will fight and protect to stay putrid. Some people don't want beauty. They are content with the monsters they create. Those are the hopeless ones. You can't save everyone. Everybody chooses his or her own life, and that is how it goes," says Linda.

"Can you help me avoid that same fate?" asks Josh.

Linda looks at him. She then smiles. "I'm not a messiah. I just don't want you or me to die without experiencing the whole side of living. No human or living thing should," Linda replies.

"Thanks for caring about me," says Josh. He brings Linda closer to him and holds her. "I was missing a person like you in my life," he says.

"I want to lie down. I'm tired," says Linda.

"Where?" asks Josh.

"By that tree," says Linda. She points to the biggest tree in the park that provided a lot of shade. It is nice, healthy, and green.

"Okay," says Josh.

They lie down under the tree and stare into each other's eyes, trying to read the other's mind and intentions. They don't know why they are staring at each other, but they don't complain about it either. I guess they are trying to find something they lacked. Linda is the first to speak.

"Josh, why the hell do you love me? I'm a defective monster. I'm a fucking evil bitch. I try to hide it, but it comes out anyway, damaging everyone near me. Afterwards, I'm left to pick up the pieces," Linda says.

"Linda, I find all of that mesmerizing. I'm not scared of your monsters. I'll even make them my pets," says Josh in a soft tone. He lightly moves some of her hair away from her face.

Linda turns from her side and on to her back. She looks up to the sky and says, "I feel like I'm losing my mind and there's nothing I can do to stop it. I feel so alone, like no one understands me or ever will. Josh, you will never comprehend this kind of empty, helpless, frustrated feeling until you have experienced it yourself. I feel like I'm slowly dying mentally. I swear, even when I fucking die I still will not have found my soul mate. I'm not going to accept to live my life with strangers like everyone else. They are so desperate to not feel alone that they will be contented with just having another physical being around," says Linda in an exasperated tone. *I want the heavens to shine down on me and steal my soul.* Linda turns back on her side and hugs Josh.

"Why does your body have to feel so comfortable and warm to me? Being next to you makes me feel kinda better. I just worry that you will become everything I hate, like poison," says Linda.

Josh looks at the sky too. "I'm glad that this empty flesh gives you some sort of comfort. My body is nothing compared to yours, Linda. Your skin feels sacred and your body is what I worship. I love it when I feel you. But anyway, I would never do anything to make you feel bad, nor would I deceive you," says Josh.

"You're a fucking liar. Love will destroy us both," Linda says.

"I'll still love you no matter what, Linda," says Josh. He turns over and kisses Linda's lips.

"I love you too," says Linda.

Josh and Linda fall asleep together on the grass under that large tree. There have no blanket to use, so they hold each other.

Chapter Thirty-One

I want to violate an angel.
I want to convert a demon.

When Linda and Josh wake up, it is evening. They must have slept for hours, maybe due to exhaustion. Life makes people tired.

"Wow, it's late," says Josh.

"Yeah," says Linda. They get up and walk to Linda's car. Before Linda gets in, Josh kisses her on the cheek.

"Good night, Linda," says Josh.

"Good night," says Linda. She drives back home. Her parents are still not home. Neither is her brother. Linda takes a shower, changes into her pajamas, and goes downstairs to watch TV. She only watches TV for thirty minutes because she hears the home phone ring from the kitchen. "Hello?" says Linda.

"Hello, this is Detective D'Angelo," says the other voice on the line.

"Hi, it's me, Linda," says Linda.

"Hi, Linda. I'm calling because we have some great news. We followed some leads, and with the help of the facial description that you gave us, we were able to catch the guy. He's in our custody now. He didn't admit to anything, but now that we got probable cause we can get his DNA and hopefully it will match the DNA from the rape kit and the fingerprints found at the scene. When we get the evidence, we'll charge him."

"I hope it does match. Did you already tell this to the Corali family?" asks Linda.

"Yes, they were very happy and relieved over the phone," says D'Angelo.

"That's good to hear, I hope it reduces their grief," says Linda.

"Me too. Besides letting you in on the good news, I was wondering if you could testify in court that she was last with him. It would support the case. Uh . . . can you do it?" asks D'Angelo.

"Of course, anything to put that psycho in jail," replies Linda.

"That's great. I'll let you know what to expect, but for now you should get some rest. You've been through quite an ordeal," replies D'Angelo.

"Yeah," says Linda.

"Have a good rest . . . bye," says D'Angelo.

"Bye," says Linda. The weight lifts off her heart. She can finally breathe. *They caught him. What a miracle.* Linda dreaded that the police would never find Jennifer's killer and that her case would have gone cold. The justice system is unstable. Many people don't receive justice for their dead. Linda is so happy she is about to cry. She hears the sound of keys at the door. Her brother and parents walk in carrying groceries and other shopping bags.

"Hi, Lynn, how was your day?" asks Mr. Cresswood.

"Great," replies Linda.

Mrs. Cresswood comes over and gives Linda a tight hug. "How's my big girl?" asks Mrs. Cresswood, as she kisses Linda on her forehead.

David walks over, sits on the couch, and begins to watch TV.

"Good, Mom. Hey, guess what?" says Linda.

"What, honey?" asks Mrs. Cresswood.

"Detective D'Angelo called," says Linda. Everyone turns around to listen to what she has to say.

"What did he say?" asks Mr. Cresswood.

"He called to say that they caught the guy. They just need to match his DNA to the crime scene in order to formally charge him," says Linda.

"Oh, that's wonderful. This is fantastic news for the Coralis," says Mr. Cresswood.

"I feel so bad that they lost their daughter," says Mrs. Cresswood, shaking her head.

"That's not all. He's not pleading guilty, so Detective D'Angelo asked if I could testify at the trial to help the case," says Linda.

"Are you going to do it?" asks David.

Linda turns to him. "Yeah," says Linda.

"Wow, Lynn, that's a big responsibility, and it won't be easy. The defense will go after you to try to discredit your testimony," says Mrs. Cresswood.

"I know, but the prosecutor will help me and prepare me for that, not to mention I'll also have some help from Detective D'Angelo," Linda says.

"I think that's a wonderful idea that you're standing up for Jennifer," says Mr. Cresswood.

"When's the trial going to take place?" asks David.

"I don't know, they'll call and let me know. Well, that's all I have to say. I'm kind of tired, so good night," says Linda.

"You're going to sleep?" asks Mrs. Cresswood.

"Yes," says Linda.

"I've got to talk to the Coralis and the other parents about this news. I bet the other parents are eager to know anything new," says Mrs. Cresswood.

Mr. Cresswood and David begin to watch football.

Linda goes upstairs and calls Samantha, Josh, and Eric. They are very happy to hear the news. They also wish her the best of luck on the trial. While she talks with Eric, there is more to the conversation.

"Linda, I feel so miserable. Why do things like this have to happen to us?" says Eric.

"You're at home, right?" asks Linda.

"No, I sneaked out. I'm here at my parents' beach house," replies Eric.

"Why are you there?" asks Linda.

"I don't know. I guess I'm waiting for you. I was just about to call you when you called me. Please come over . . . I really need somebody, and you're just the right person," replies Eric.

Hmm . . . Eric is putting me in an awkward situation, but I don't want him to hurt himself or something. "Okay, I'll be there in an hour," says Linda before she hangs up.

She changes, does her hair and makeup and sneaks out from her window. She did not want her family asking questions about where she is going. Linda knew where the beach house was. She, Eric, Samantha, Jennifer, and Josh hung out there every other summer. Linda climbs down the thick, sturdy vines that grew right by her bedroom window. Linda drops down on the grass and quickly runs to her car. She is glad that she parked a little far from her house or her family would hear her car start up. Linda gets into her car and drives off toward the beach house. She hopes nobody will find out that she is gone. *Isn't Eric worried about his parents finding out that he's not home either?*

After some driving, she pulls up onto the beach house driveway. She turns off her headlights and takes out her keys from the ignition. She locks up her car and walks up to the house. She sees that the door is slightly ajar. She opens it and closes it behind her. It is dark in the house, except for some lights that are on toward the back. She walks toward the patio.

Linda sees that Eric is sitting on the edge of the patio floor staring out to the ocean.

"Eric?" says Linda.

"Huh?" says Eric. He awakens from his thoughts and turns around.

"The door was open," says Linda.

"I left it open for you," says Eric.

Linda looks at him.

"Come here, and sit down," Eric says with a smile.

"Are you okay?" asks Linda.

"No," says Eric.

"Eric, what can I do to fix you?" Linda sighs.

"Just stay with me," says Eric.

"Jennifer's death has not only affected you but everyone else too. Everything is stressing me out enough. Now you got me worried about you too," says Linda.

Eric looks at Linda. "You actually care about me?" he asks.

"Of course I do. I love that you want me to be by your side. I love you as a friend and what you contain within," says Linda.

"Linda, I know that you and Josh really like each other," says Eric as he looks at her.

"We're not a couple," replies Linda.

"I can see he really cares about you," says Eric.

"Listen, I'm not a relationship type of person. My brain is going a million miles an hour and I'm lost within the mazes of my head. I can't even be committed to myself, let alone with others," says Linda.

"I know just what you mean. Linda. When did you steal a part of my soul?" asks Eric, laughing.

"That hardly means we're meant for each other," she says, smiling.

"Fuck fate. If life is predestined, what's the point of living?" asks Eric.

Linda looks at Eric. "Life is mostly about enduring. You've got to create what you want because life will offer you nothing," replies Linda.

Eric nods. He stares back out to the ocean.

"Eric, why are you avoiding Samantha, after you had sex with her?" asks Linda.

The statement surprises Eric. There is silence. Eric then sighs. "So she told you. I am not mad at her. She was bound to tell someone, and you are her friend," says Eric.

"Well?" Linda says.

"I don't know. I was drunk; she was drunk. We were both trying to comprehend the death of Jennifer. It was not supposed to happen, and I feel somewhat evil about it. I don't want her to feel like I used her or anything. It's just that I feel nothing for Samantha. Now, I just feel uncomfortable being around her. Relationships don't work with me. I got to deal with this problem myself, and I don't want to hurt her any further . . . I mean I told her this when we started making out. She said she was okay with it. I guess we both didn't understand the reality or how it would impact us later," says Eric.

"You should have been smarter. I don't like the way you just tossed Samantha to the side like that and how quickly you forgot about Jennifer," Linda says angrily.

Eric looks at Linda. "Linda, please don't be mad with me. I couldn't handle you being angry with me. Please. I would kill myself if you were to walk away from me and hate me," says Eric, as his eyes get watery.

"Don't try to blackmail me emotionally! Why did you ask me over here? What do you want? Sex? Is that your goal, to get any stupid girl to sleep with you? What do you want? Do you want to use me for sex, too? You know what? You're nothing to me! I hate you!" Linda yells as she turns around to walk out of the house.

Eric gets up, runs to her, and stops her. "No, Linda, it's not like that. I really respect you. Linda, please let me explain. You're the only girl I know who truly understands me. Please don't act this way. Listen, if you hate me right now just hit me, but don't be angry with me. Here, hit me," says Eric as he walks in front of Linda and closes his eyes.

"You want me to hit you?" asks Linda.

"Go ahead," says Eric.

"You deserve it, because you can be a real jerk," says Linda. Linda lifts her hand, pauses and slaps Eric hard with the back of her hand.

Eric breathes deeply. The side of his face is very red. He opens his eyes. "Are you still mad at me?" asks Eric, looking deeply into her eyes in his anguish.

"No, not anymore. It was kind of therapeutic. Consider it a paid debt," sighs Linda.

"Linda, I promise that I'll call Samantha and apologize to her and tell her why I acted the way I did," says Eric.

"That's a good idea," says Linda. She walks over to the kitchen and takes a bottle of red wine from the wine rack on the counter. She pops it open with a cork opener and gulps some down. "Here, do you want some?" asks Linda.

"Yes," says Eric. Linda walks over to Eric. He takes the bottle and gulps some wine down as well. Linda walks out on to the patio and down onto the beach. Eric follows her as she walks toward the tide. She takes off her shoes, rolls up her pants, and lets the tide wash over her feet.

"What's the purpose of life?" asks Linda, suddenly breaking the silence. "I don't want to sound cliché, but sometimes I really wonder about it."

"Yeah, that's a question I wonder about, too. Another thing is, why are human beings so unsatisfied with everything? Why is it so hard for us to be content? It seems like we have to strain to manufacture our happiness. I don't know. I can't function how society is telling me to function. I feel like people are restricting me, keeping me enclosed, and I'm not free to be myself. Sometimes I feel like I just don't belong on this planet," replies Eric.

"I get more attracted to you every time you speak 'cause I feel the same way. In our madness we have some sort of comprehension of each other on why we act the way we do. Please pass the bottle," says Linda.

Eric passes the bottle. She sips and stares out at the ocean as if she is waiting for the arrival of her mental peace. *I really want serenity within myself. I want to understand everything that I can't comprehend. I don't want my mind to be a battlefield. Illumination is hiding from me.*

"You have a beautiful voice and ideology, Linda. I wish I could take our souls to another world where we could have everything our minds are dying for," says Eric.

Linda is still staring at the ocean. "How do we get there? This human life only offers split-second emotions from that world in a substitute form. I just want to actually have the opportunity to live there and enjoy it," replies Linda.

Eric turns his head to look at Linda. "The most difficult part is to find it and stay there," he says.

The moonlight shines on them. They look ghostlike, nonexistent in gray. Linda picks up her shoes and walks back to the patio of the house. Eric follows. She and Eric wash off their feet and get the sand off their shoes.

CHAPTER THIRTY-TWO

As they enter the house again, Linda sips out of the bottle. She hands the bottle back to Eric. Linda hardly cares about anything at this point including the potential germs from bottle sharing.

Eric gulps down more wine. He starts to feel just a little bit of the alcoholic effects. The bottle is almost finished and they had not eaten anything.

Linda is feeling the light effects of alcohol as well. "Tell me that you won't ever kill yourself. Can you please just promise me on that one?" says Linda.

Eric looks deeply into her eyes. "So you care about me that much?" asks Eric.

"If you go and do that, it will destroy me," says Linda.

"I would never want to do anything that would hurt you. I love you more than anything. It's okay if you don't believe me. After what I did to Samantha, you probably think I'm a womanizer, and I am. However, I don't know why I feel the way I do. There is something about you that I haven't found in Samantha, Jennifer, or any other girl, that makes me so attracted to you. I just have a crazy desire to want to do everything to make you happy. I never felt like this before," says Eric.

Linda does not say anything.

Eric looks intently into Linda's eyes. "Linda, can I kiss you?" asks Eric.

"What is it about alcohol that makes you so amorous with every girl that's next to you?" asks Linda. *Why do all my guy friends want to be with me now? Eric's girlfriend just died. Why is he moving on so quickly? He must be crazy. The whole situation is stupid. Nothing makes sense in this world.*

"Trust me, it's not the alcohol, and I'm not drunk," says Eric as he leans in closer.

"Fine, whatever," says Linda.

Eric lightly nibbles her lip as he begins kissing her softly. Gradually the kissing becomes more forceful, and Linda falls back against the wall.

Eric whispers in her ear, "I wanted to feel you for a long time. Linda, when I look at you, I feel as if you're a part of me."

Linda pulls Eric's hair and kisses back with the same force. They both feel each other's tongue. Eric pulls Linda's body closer to his as both of his hands grab her ass. Eric licks and bites her neck. Linda nibbles his lip. Eric nibbles her tongue. He kisses her out of hunger. They move through hell, heaven, and earth, and cannot see past the blinding, rushing colors.

"I'm fucked up. I will never be me. Stay here and save me," says Eric. He suddenly stops kissing her and holds her.

Linda sees the tears come out of his eyes. His face looks like he has met death. Linda licks his tears. She kisses his cheek.

Eric buries his face in her neck. He just wants to feel her safety, her warmth. He wants to breathe her in. "You taste more delicious than I could have ever imagined," says Eric as he whispers into her ear. He then looks into Linda's eyes. "Come here, I've got something to show you."

He walks her to another room, a studio. When he opens the door, Linda is surprised. In this room are many beautiful paintings hanging around. It looked like a gallery. "I didn't know you painted," says Linda.

"Do you want to paint with me?" asks Eric. His face looks like it is begging for approval.

"Yes, of course," says Linda.

They get the paintbrushes out, a huge canvas, and a lot of paint cans. They go to the other side of the room where they can paint without ruining the other paintings. They start to paint abstractly this time, throwing and splattering paint on the large canvas. They laugh as they throw the paint on the canvas and on each other. They did not care if the paint might ruin their clothes. Deep, rich, beautiful colors fill the canvas. When they finish, they are both out of breath. They lie down on the hard floor and breathe heavily. They face each other as they lay on their side.

"I think we made a beautiful canvas," says Eric.

"So do I," says Linda.

"You got a lot of paint on you," says Eric.

"And so do you," says Linda.

Eric moves over and is directly above Linda. He doesn't say anything; neither does Linda. "Do you mind if I remove your clothes?" asks Eric.

"No, it's fine. Go ahead, discover it," says Linda.

Eric gets some scissors from the table. He slowly begins to cut Linda's shirt off starting at the bottom middle of the shirt, cutting straight up. He then cuts and removes the remains of her shirt completely. Her skin, bra, and stomach are exposed. Eric bends down and kisses Linda fervently. His tongue travels down her neck past her chest and across her cleavage. He licks her stomach and sucks and kisses her navel. He unbuttons her pants and removes it. Now her underwear is exposed too. Eric goes on to gently use his teeth as he bites and licks various parts of her body.

He whispers into her ear, "I love your sexy bra and underwear. Why does everything about you have to be perfect?" His hands feel the smooth softness of her legs. "I never felt any girl's skin as amazing as yours. That's because you're truly beautiful; you carry it in your genes," says Eric. He kisses and licks her legs starting from her thighs and down to her ankles.

Linda sits up. "I like the way you bite. You're unsystematic," she says, and laughs.

"It gets better," Eric says with a smile. He begins to massage her back.

"That feels amazing," says Linda.

"Perfect, because that's how I want you to feel," says Eric as he kisses her neck. He works all the right spots where the back muscles are tense. He moves in front of her, grabs hold of her foot, and begins to massage it.

"You're really nice," Linda says with a laugh.

"Thanks. And your skin tastes lovely," says Eric.

"Really?" Linda laughs.

"Yeah, compared to all the other girls I've been with," says Eric.

"Okay . . ." says Linda.

"You're a goddess. You've been around me for years, and I never knew it," says Eric as he switches to her other foot.

"Shut up," Linda retorts with a laugh.

"For real. I'm going to get my own place just so that I can watch you walk around in lingerie all the time," and Eric laughs too.

"You're insane. Who the fuck said I would do that?" She laughs again.

Eric smiles and says, "Me." He then stops massaging her foot and sighs as he looks at the floor. "Linda, I want to fuck you really badly, but I'm not going to. You are so much more than that. You transcend to the beyond," says Eric.

Linda looks at him. "Thank you for respecting me . . . it makes me feel less inferior. Now, I'll just have to play with you instead, so take off your shirt because I want to see what you're hiding," says Linda.

"Let's be fair; you take it off," he says and smiles.

Linda grabs hold of his shirt and takes it up and off over his head. Linda grabs his wrist and looks at his biceps as she feels them with her fingers and says, "Your skin is soft but your muscles are hard."

"My body is your playground," says Eric. Linda begins to lick, kiss and bite his neck, shoulders and arms.

Her fingers explore his throat area and travel across his bare chest. "You're flat-chested," Linda observes, with a laugh.

"Yes, I know. I'm so devastated that I'm getting a boob job next week," says Eric. They laugh.

Linda lightly pokes his abs. "I bet your organs are real soft," says Linda.

"Maybe they are," says Eric.

"Is it okay if I remove your pants?" asks Linda.

"Okay with me," says Eric.

Linda removes his pants along with his shoes. "So you wear boxers, huh?" says Linda.

"I go either way, boxers, briefs. Who gives a shit; we're all going to die anyway," says Eric.

"True," Linda replies with a laugh. She lifts one of his legs up a bit. "Your legs are heavy. You also have very clean, healthy feet."

"Thanks. I do my best to be my best," replies Eric.

Linda rests her ear on Eric's naked chest.

Eric holds her in his arms and rests his hands on her back.

"I can hear your heart beat and your lungs opening and closing," says Linda.

"Does that mean I'm not fake?" asks Eric.

Linda puts her fingers though his soft hair and gives him a tongue kiss. "You're no one's property. Remember that," says Linda as she rolls away to her side.

Eric turns over too and places his hand on her shoulder. It travels down her arm, over the edges of her stomach, butt, and thigh. It travels back up to rest on the edge of her stomach. "Has anyone told you that you have a beautiful body?" Eric asks.

"Yes," Linda replies. There is silence.

"Linda, why do you make me want you?" asks Eric.

"It's all in your head," replies Linda.

Eric looks up at the ceiling. "That's where all the issues lie," says Eric.

"We should clean the place up, it's a mess," says Linda as she gets up.

"Yeah, that's right," says Eric.

They put their clothes back on and spend thirty minutes cleaning up the mess they made. As they finish Linda says, "I didn't notice that I really do have a lot of paint on me."

"Why don't we put our clothes in the washer and that way you can take a shower?" asks Eric.

"You cut up my shirt, so what am I going to wear?" Linda asks.

"Sorry about that. I think I've got a T-shirt around here that might fit you. There's a bathrobe in the bathroom upstairs. You can wear it while we wait for our clothes to dry," says Eric.

"What about you?" asks Linda.

"I'm going to use the downstairs bathroom. I have some clean clothes here," says Eric.

"Okay, everything is set?" asks Linda.

"Yes," replies Eric.

Linda goes upstairs and changes into the bathrobe. She walks back downstairs to the washing room and puts her clothes in the washer. She goes back upstairs to take her shower.

Eric finds a robe downstairs. He changes into it and put his clothes in the same washer. He adds the soap and starts the wash. He goes into his room to find a shirt for Linda. He finds a black T-shirt that had shrunk in the wash that he forgot to throw out. He walks back to the empty bathroom to take his shower. For twenty minutes, the house is quiet, except for the sound of separate showers going.

Chapter Thirty-Three

Eric is the first to finish. He puts on his new pair of clothes and goes back to the washer to put the clothes from the washer into the dryer. He also adds some fabric softener sheets. Ten minutes later Linda steps out of the shower, towels off, and puts the robe back on. She hears a knock at the door.

"Linda?" asks Eric.

"Yes?" replies Linda.

"Your clothes are ready. I'm going to leave them on this small table by the door, okay?" says Eric.

"Okay," Linda says. She hears him walk away. She opens the door and picks up her folded clothes from the table and goes back into the bathroom. She changes into them and walks downstairs.

Eric is in the kitchen eating. On the kitchen counter there is a plate with a ham, lettuce, and cheese sandwich on it. A bottle of water is right next to it. "I made some food for you," says Eric.

"You're so sweet," says Linda. She sits down on a chair by the counter. She bites into the sandwich and begins to eat it.

"Does it taste good?" asks Eric.

"Yes, it does," replies Linda.

Eric looks at Linda. "You look pretty when you're eating," says Eric, smiling.

Linda stops eating to contain her laugh. "Eric, do you know what you want out of life?" she asks.

"No, I've haven't a clue," replies Eric.

Linda stares at the kitchen wall. "I'm sorry, Eric. All I have been doing is asking too many questions. Sometimes I wish I were stupid because you don't notice all the monsters lurking about or the danger of them coming to destroy you. Nothing matters, everything is wonderful."

"Linda, you seem to forget that those people are like dead goldfish in a fishbowl. They have lost everything that makes them shine. They are dead inside. Walking zombies whose hearts and minds are filled with every dirty thing that epitomizes the word repulsive. The question is do you want to be the walking dead or alive?" Eric asks.

"Alive, of course," says Linda.

"You have awareness. Very few people are conscious of their surroundings or what kind of people they are. They will never be happy. Awareness allows you to explore a beauty to life that you cannot see when you are asleep," says Eric.

"I hunger for beauty. I guess I just want to live in a world where the impossible can happen because the world I live in is so ugly, boring, and repetitive. I yearn for something else, something new, and something I haven't experienced before," replies Linda as she stares off into the distance.

"Those are some hard feelings to deal with," says Eric.

"Have you ever felt so tired that no matter what you did it would not go away? A sort of exhaustion that makes you feel like you're living on autopilot, and the people around you just feel like they're part of the scenery, kind of like props during a theatrical performance," Linda says. She sighs and continues, "Why are human beings' intentions mostly evil? Why are we deceptive in our manners? Why do we always want to outshine the other? Why is life just a competition of money and class? Why do human beings do horrible things to each other? We don't care about anyone or anything on this planet. Why are we so narcissistic and selfish? Why are we so obsessed with appearances? I just don't want to stay on this planet anymore. I don't understand people and neither do they about me. Eric . . . I'm so tired I feel drained," says Linda.

"You have friends who care about you. I care about you and I understand what you are feeling, that's why I want to be close to you. I want to learn more about you and from you," replies Eric.

Linda finishes her sandwich and so does Eric. "Do you think about all those things often?" asks Eric.

"Every day; how can I not? I'm reminded about it constantly," says Linda as she opens her water bottle.

"Your mind is a combat zone worse than mine," says Eric as Linda drinks from her water bottle. She finishes it.

"Well, I guess I should be going," says Linda.

"Already?" asks Eric.

"Yes," says Linda.

"Do you want me to walk you to your car?" asks Eric.

"No, that's fine," says Linda.

"Okay. I'm really glad I got to spend some time with you," says Eric.

"No problem," says Linda. She gets up, says her goodbyes, and walks down the hall to the front door.

Eric is still in the kitchen. Something does not feel right to him. It is quiet. He does not hear a car turn on or drive off. *I want to be sure that she got to her car okay.*

Eric leaves the kitchen and makes his way to the front door. He walks down the hall, but before he gets to the door, Eric hears something to the left, which is another living room. Eric is surprised when he sees that Linda is lying collapsed on the floor with her face on her arms. Her hair looks a mess, and she is crying uncontrollably. It sounds very painful. It's as if her soul is crying.

Eric does not know how to react for a second. *Maybe she is having a mental break down like I did.* He runs over to her, kneels down, turns her over, and lifts her head off the floor.

She covers her hands with her face. "I just can't take it anymore. I hate people. I hate myself. I hate the world. I hate everything. I just can't . . . it's too painful . . . having to endure," says Linda.

He holds her as she buries her face into his chest, crying. "It's okay. I'm here. Relax. Everything is going to be fine. I love you," says Eric as he caresses her back.

After a few minutes, Linda runs out of tears. She lifts her head from his chest and looks at him. Her eyes look empty, red, and puffy. "You must think I'm crazy. I'm sorry that I'm scaring you. That's what I do best. Scare people away," says Linda in an awkward, post-crying voice.

"I would never judge or reject you. I'm going through the same miserable shit too," replies Eric.

Linda gets up. "Okay. This time I'll make it to my car," she says, trying to regain her composure.

Eric catches her just as she stumbles. "There is no way I'm letting you drive feeling like this. Here, I'll take you to my parents' room because it's bigger and you'll get a nice breeze through there," says Eric.

Linda is not even listening, because she has fallen asleep in his arms. She is exhausted. He picks her up, carries her upstairs, and lays her down on the bed. He covers her with blankets. He looks at her and feels her forehead to see if she is coming down with a fever or something. Her eyes are closed. Eric reaches to shut off the lamp and then walk out of the room when Linda grabs hold of his arm. Eric is surprised that she is awake now.

"Stay," says Linda. Her eyes are open now.

"Are you going to be okay?" asks Eric.

"Yes. Stay," Linda repeats.

"You don't have to ask twice. You know I would never make you feel lonely," says Eric. He walks around to the opposite side of the bed and gets under the covers with Linda. She turns over and hugs him like a stuffed animal. Eric puts his arm around her shoulder. He can hear her soft breathing and feel her heartbeat. He kisses the top of her head. *Why are we human beings so complicated?* Eric wonders. Not long later he falls asleep.

Hours go by as celestial beings use the black canvas of the sky as a stage. Slowly, luminosity creeps up, threatening to steal the area with a new set of friends. Linda wakes up to the smell of ocean water. She looks at the clock. It reads 5:00 a.m. She looks around and suddenly remembers where she is. She sees Eric sleeping next to her. He looks very peaceful and beautiful. She realizes that she has to get back home before her parents find out that she is gone. She looks at Eric and kisses him on one of his eyelids. She gets out of the bed, takes a sticky note and pen from the nightstand, and writes a note saying that she is going back home. She places it where Eric can find it, on the side of the lamp facing the bed. She walks downstairs. She gets her stuff, walks out the door, gets into her car, and drives off.

When she arrives home, she parks her car away from her house. She cannot walk through the front door; it is too much of a risk. Her family might hear her and start asking questions about where she was. She decides to climb back up the vines. Her bedroom window is still unlocked. She pulls open the window and climbs back in. She is tired. She brushes her teeth, changes back into her pajamas, and falls asleep on her bed.

Eric wakes up to the sound of seagulls. He looks at the clock. It is 7:00 a.m. He looks around and realizes that Linda is gone. *Where did she go?* He sees the sticky note on the lamp. He takes it off and reads it. *She went back home*, Eric says to himself. Now he has to think about getting back home discreetly, too.

CHAPTER THIRTY-FOUR

I feel so much . . . anguish . . . inside.
Must . . . fly.

It is about 3:00 p.m. Samantha is in her house watching TV. When she hears the phone ring, she walks to her living room and picks it up. "Hello?"

"Is this Samantha?"

"Who is this?" asks Samantha.

"It's Eric."

"Oh . . . hi, Eric," Samantha says.

"Hi, Samantha. I'm just calling to say that I'm sorry . . . .

Linda is baking a chocolate cake. *I love chocolate. I like the reaction that takes place as you eat it. It's a sudden explosion of taste and pleasure. Like a little piece of true happiness.* Anyway, she is mixing the batter when she hears the phone ring. *Why are there so many phone calls?* She sighs, stops what she is doing, and picks up the phone. "Hello?"

"Linda?"

"Yes, that's me," Linda replies.

"It's Samantha. Guess what? The strangest thing happened."

"What?" asks Linda?

"I just got off the phone with Eric. He called to apologize and explain why he's been avoiding me. He told me about his problems. He also told me that he asked you to slap him because you were mad that he ignored me and forgot about Jennifer after what happened. Did you really slap him?" asks Samantha.

"Yes, I met up with him, so that we could talk about all the shit that was happening around us. He made me mad and, so when he asked me to, I did. He deserved it 'cause he can be so selfish sometimes. What he did was messed up," says Linda.

"Wow, thanks for doing that and for making him realize he needed to apologize," says Samantha.

"No problem," says Linda.

"Thanks for caring about me," says Samantha.

"Of course. I will always be there for you. So, are you guys past this issue?" asks Linda.

"Yes, we decided to go our separate ways. We're not going to hang out with each other anymore because it's just too awkward and uncomfortable for us," says Samantha.

"Hmm . . . well, if that's the conclusion then we've just got to deal," says Linda.

"Yes," says Samantha.

Why are human beings so problematic? Linda wonders.

"What are you doing?" asks Samantha.

"Baking a chocolate cake with frosting," replies Linda.

"That sounds delicious. Can you save me a piece?" asks Samantha.

"Yes, of course. Why don't you come over here in about forty minutes, and it should be ready," says Linda.

"That sounds great. I'll be there," says Samantha.

"Okay, see you then. Bye," says Linda.

"Bye," says Samantha.

Linda hangs up the phone. She goes back to mixing her batter. She coats a baking pan with some nonstick cooking spray. She pours all the batter into it. The oven is already preheated. She opens the oven door and places it inside. She sets the timer for thirty-five minutes. She washes her hands and walks over to the counter. She starts to read a book as she waits for the cake to bake.

Thirty-five minutes later, she hears the timer and pulls the cake out of the oven. The cake is moist and smells heavenly. Linda grabs the frosting container, opens it, and applies the frosting with a butter knife. When she finishes applying the frosting, she covers it with a very light cloth. Seven minutes later, Linda hears the doorbell ring. She opens the door.

"Hi," says Samantha.

"Hi, come in," says Linda.

"It smells so good in here," says Samantha.

"Yeah, I just finished. It's lying on the counter," says Linda.

Samantha walks over to the counter and peeks under the cloth. "It looks so good, too," says Samantha.

"Let me cut you a slice," says Linda. She walks back into the kitchen, opens a drawer, and takes out a knife. Linda removes the light cloth, cuts Samantha a slice, and puts it on a plate with a fork.

Samantha takes a bite. "This is so freaking good!" she says.

"I'm glad you like it. Let's sit on the couch," says Linda. She cuts herself a piece of cake, too. They sit down on the couch. "So how's life treating you today?" asks Linda.

"I guess our moods depend on whether life does or does not want to be a bitch today," says Samantha.

"So true," says Linda.

"Well, I guess happy, 'cause I'm here with you eating some damn good cake," says Samantha.

Linda laughs.

"School's coming up," says Samantha.

"I know. Summer's drawing to a close," Linda sighs.

"Linda?" asks Samantha.

"Yes?"

"Do you think we will ever get over the Jennifer thing?" asks Samantha.

"I don't know how you or the others feel, but I think this emptiness is going to stay with me for a while, and no matter what I do it will always come back and remind me," says Linda, her eyes looking off into the distance.

"She meant a lot to us. How could it not affect us so badly?" replies Samantha.

"Do you want to watch TV?" asks Linda.

"Yes, let's try to find a movie," says Samantha.

Linda grabs the remote and turns on the huge flat-screen. Right away, they hear the theater sound system. After a few minutes of channel surfing, they settle on a thriller. Linda brings out some sodas with ice and some popcorn. For four hours, they are problem free.

CHAPTER THIRTY-FIVE

Linda wakes up at ten o' clock in the morning. She gets out of bed. While she is getting dressed, she remembers all the good times that Jennifer and she had. Linda also remembers how happy Samantha looked when she said goodbye to her last night. All Linda wanted is for her friends to be happy.

Linda hears her cell ring and picks up her phone. "Hello?"

"Hey, it's me Josh."

Again, thinks Linda. "Hi, what are you up to?" asks Linda.

"I was going to ask you the same thing," says Josh. "I want to see you."

"Aren't you tired of seeing me?" asks Linda.

"I would never tire of seeing your beautiful face," says Josh.

"Cut the sappiness," Linda says, laughing. Josh laughs too.

"For real, do you want to go for a walk or something?" asks Josh.

"Um . . . okay," Linda says.

"I'll meet you at your house at eleven-thirty. Bye," says Josh.

"Okay, bye," says Linda. She finishes getting ready, and Josh arrives at her house on time. Linda is waiting on the steps.

"Wow, you look more beautiful every time I see you," says Josh.

"You too," replies Linda.

They start walking arm and arm down the street. "Where do you want to go?" asks Josh.

"How about into town?" asks Linda.

"That sounds good. Maybe if we get hungry, we can get something to eat," says Josh.

"Yeah," replies Linda.

"Did you eat breakfast?" asks Josh.

"Yes, I did, and you?" asks Linda.

"Yeah," replies Josh.

"So it's settled. We're not hungry right now," says Linda.

"Yes," says Josh as he smiles at Linda.

Linda and Josh walk closer to town. "It's a beautiful day," says Linda.

"Yes, it is," replies Josh.

When they arrive in town, they decide to get some coffee. They both order light coffee and bagels with cream cheese. "So what do you want to talk about?" asks Josh.

"Absolutely nothing. I'm tired of talking," says Linda.

"That's true; sometimes silence is the most beautiful thing in the world," says Josh.

"It depends on the situation," says Linda.

"Yeah," says Josh. They start to eat their bagels. They are quiet for about seven minutes and they enjoy every minute of it. "You want to go look at more stuff?" asks Josh.

"Yeah," says Linda. They throw away their trash and begin walking. "I want to buy some breath mints," says Linda.

"Okay," Josh says. They walk into a liquor store, and Linda gets her mints. When she arrives at the register and is about to pay, Josh provides the money to the cashier before she can. Linda looks at Josh quizzically. He gives her a quick wink. Linda smiles and shakes her head. When they walk out, they share the mint pack. They start walking down the streets again arm in arm.

"Josh, I need you so much right now. I'm really scared of myself. I feel like my brain is trying to kill me. Tell me that you trust me," says Linda.

She holds on to Josh as if the universe will cease to exist if she lets go. Everything would evaporate and drain away to make room for other people. *I do not want to be at fault for destroying a beautiful occurrence,* Linda thinks. *How I hate and love everything at the same time. There are so many emotions going through me that I feel like I want to explode and relieve the pressure.*

"Josh, I'm tired of these meetings. You should stay away from me. I don't want to hurt or trouble you. You deserve a common girl. Someone who is simple in her thinking and not so fucked up like me. Don't torture yourself, run away from me. Please, I don't want your life to be miserable like mine," says Linda.

"Linda, I do trust you, and your life is not miserable. It's the most beautiful thing I've encountered. Anyway, I don't want a simple, stupid Barbie doll for company. How many times do I have to tell you that you can't get rid of me that easily? Linda, all I ask is for you to love me and invite me into your life as a boyfriend," says Josh.

"Josh, my life is both beautiful and ugly. My personality is just scary and unstable. You don't even want to know the shit that I think about."

"Linda, I'm not scared of your thinking. I actually love it. I love who you are, and I love what you do. I have no qualms. Linda, I just love you, okay?"

"But, I still don't understand why you feel love toward me," says Linda.

"Why? The answer is simple. It's everything that makes you, you," says Josh.

Linda lets out a deep breath. "Fine . . . you can be . . . my boyfriend," she says.

Josh is ecstatic. "Thank you so much," he says as he kisses Linda on the cheek. "All I ever wanted was for you to be my girl."

"Now, you're my main squeeze," says Linda with a laugh. They start walking past some stores. When they pass a flower shop, Josh takes three roses and gives them to her. Linda gives him a *what are you doing?* look. "You've got to pay for those," says Linda.

"Just keep walking," says Josh with a smile.

"Hey, where you going? You gotta pay," says the shopkeeper.

Josh grabs Linda's hand. "Let's go," Josh says.

They run out of there so fast. They can hear the shopkeeper yell after them. They run through the streets. Josh points to a field not far off, away from town. They never ran so hard in their lives. They start running through the fields. The dry grass is up to their thighs. They then stop.

"Josh what were you thinking? For a couple of measly roses, you're going to get us in trouble," Linda says. They are breathing heavily.

"If they're just some measly roses then it shouldn't be a problem," says Josh.

"I love your atmosphere," replies Linda. She kisses him.

Josh lays her on the ground, in a clearing, where there is fresh grass.

"What a place," says Linda as she looks around.

"Yeah, that's true," replies Josh. They kiss, laugh, and roll away from the opening and into the tall grass.

Their world is a mixture of deep space and life's coveting. The light that falls on them is so bright that it exposes and burns all their demons. Linda touches Josh's face. The bright light accentuates his face in a way that makes him look angelic.

Josh takes hold of her hand and kisses the bottom of her wrist. "I want to be yours, Linda. I don't want there to be someone else," says Josh.

"You want it to be just us?" asks Linda.

"Yes," says Josh.

"Hmm . . . . Let me think about that . . . . Okay then," says Linda.

"You worried me there for a minute," says Josh with a laugh. He lies on his back. They look at the clear blue sky.

"Do you ever wonder what our purpose is on this planet?" asks Linda.

"Yes," replies Josh.

"Sometimes I become aware that I'm alive. It then scares me because I realize that I have sole responsibility of taking care of this body. Then I think about getting old, and I wonder how it's going to feel to die. Everything that has a beginning has an end," says Linda.

Josh looks at Linda. "That realization scares me right now," says Josh. He moves closer to Linda. "Don't worry about anything, because I'm here," he says.

He kisses Linda's lips and runs his hands through her silky hair. Since she is wearing a tank top and shorts, he kisses her cleavage and feels the insides of her thighs. Her skin feels warm and soft on his fingertips. As they roll through the grass, kissing again, he feels her ass. "Linda, everything about you shocks my insides," Josh says.

"Okay, now get off, you filthy animal." Linda laughs as she pushes him off and sits up.

"Sorry, but you're just so irresistible," replies Josh. He gets closer behind her and lightly bites her neck.

"Anyway, what time is it?" asks Linda.

Josh looks at his cell. "About three o'clock."

"Do you want to go back to harsh reality or stay in bliss here for a little longer?" asks Linda.

"What do you think?" Josh smiles as he kisses Linda's neck. "I wish life always felt this peaceful."

"This grass is itchy," says Linda.

"You're right, I guess good moments are not meant to last forever. There's always a consequence," says Josh.

"Yes," says Linda.

When Linda gets up, Josh picks her up and swings her in circles as he carries her. Linda laughs and says, "Let me down, you crazy weirdo." Josh sets her down.

"I enjoyed that," says Linda.

"I will make your life as fun as possible. I promise," says Josh.

Linda attacks Josh with a hug. "I love you so much. You're my anti-depressant."

"I love you too, because you're my morphine," replies Josh.

They walk out of the grass and leave the roses behind. "Now we have to avoid that rose stand for our whole lives," Linda says with a smile.

Josh laughs. "If that's so, then so be it."

Instead of going through town, they decide to go around it and enjoy the natural scenery. They can hear different species of birds chirping. "Doesn't that sound beautiful?" asks Josh.

"Yes, very unique and wonderful to hear," replies Linda.

As they walk into the neighborhood, Josh stops and hugs her. Linda hugs him back.

"Linda, you make me feel so good. Sometimes I don't want to let you go because I'm scared something might happen to you and that I may never see you again," says Josh.

"Don't worry, I'll never let you go, or abandon you without proper notice," says Linda.

"I know, but I just want to have enough time to fully appreciate you," says Josh. They stop embracing and continue to walk.

"Josh, don't you want to do something that is going to change the world? Don't you want to create something that will make you feel redeemed? I don't know; sometimes I'm scared that I might die and not accomplish anything. I want to be remembered for something, so that I can feel that my existence was not just to use up air," says Linda.

"Linda, I can see that you want to do impressive things. How can you not? With a personality like yours, the sky's the limit. However, you already branded yourself on me. I just want to say thanks for fixing me. Maybe that can count as a good deed," says Josh.

"Thanks," says Linda.

When they arrive at Linda's house, Josh does not want to leave her. "Look what you've done to me. I am officially your marionette," says Josh sheepishly.

"You're so cute," says Linda. "Don't worry. I'll be fine on my own. My house is just four feet ahead," says Linda as she smiles.

"One last kiss, please?" says Josh.

Linda kisses him on the lips. He heals her and she heals him.

"Remember that I'll always be there to protect you, because I love you. You can't imagine to what depths," says Josh.

"Yes, I know. I love you, too. Now get some rest," says Linda.

They say their goodbyes and Linda walks back in to her house. *I feel like his heart is in my hands. I don't like that kind of feeling. How can days and hours make so many changes in one's life? One planet, but billions upon billions of stories are each occurring at a different place and time.*

Chapter Thirty-Six

It is a beautiful Saturday afternoon in Josewood. A bunch of high, drunk, and rich white kids speed through the streets of Josewood in a red Ferrari.

Linda is doing some shopping for her first year at the university. *What I hate the most is wasting too much money on insignificant things. However, I need new clothes, so it's rational.*

Okay, that's the last of it, Linda says to herself as she walks out of a clothing store called Clouds. Linda begins to walk home. She bought all her school supplies as well as new clothes today. She waits for the pedestrian light to come on. When it does, she starts to cross. As she is crossing, flashbacks of the road trip enter her mind. She cannot believe her best friend is dead. Jennifer's funeral is two days from now. She cannot cry now because all her tears are gone. The incident left an empty space in her soul. All the emotional baggage arrives when she remembers. *I don't want to stress out or get depressed again.* She takes a deep breath.

"Dude, I think you should pull over. It's dangerous to drive like this," says Rodney, who is inebriated in the passenger seat of the red Ferrari.

"That's true, it's scientifically proven," says Jeff in the back seat with a drunken slur as he passes out.

"It's my fucking Ferrari. I'll do what I want!" says Will. He starts to search for his dope, thinking it probably fell under the driver's seat. He takes his eyes off the road.

"Watch out!" screams Rodney. However, his reaction time is distorted and slow.

The front of the car smashes into Linda, as her head and body then smash into the windshield. She slides off the car and back onto the pavement. The car rolls to a stop. People and witnesses scream and rush to the scene. Someone calls an ambulance. The witnesses detain the drunken and drugged-out driver and passengers of the Ferrari.

"I didn't want this to happen. I'm sorry, oh my God!" says Will repeatedly.

"I didn't do anything. I don't want to go to jail," Rodney and Jeff frantically say to the people standing around. All three of them look anxious and look as if they might throw up.

Sirens of the approaching ambulance and police cars fill the air. There is a lot of blood and glass at the scene. When the paramedics arrive, they check Linda's pulse. It is beating, but barely. Rodney, Will, and Jeff get their injuries checked on by one of the paramedics. They have minor cuts and bruises.

The police quickly question them and search their vehicle. The police arrest them and pin them with serious charges.

Josh is outside with some other guy friends when he hears all the commotion way up the street. He and his friends decide to check it out. When they arrive, they see a lot of people. Josh decides to squeeze through. What he sees almost stops his heart from beating.

"Oh my God, Linda!" Josh screams as he tries to rush to her side, but the police stop him because he is hysterical and they do not know who he is. The paramedics put Linda on a stretcher.

"Let me see her! Please, I'm her boyfriend!" screams Josh. By now tears are streaming down his face. They let him through. He rushes into the ambulance and explains himself to the paramedics. They agree to let him be by Linda's side as they rush her to the hospital.

He grabs hold of her hand. "Linda, please don't die. I love you too much . . . please," Josh cries. "Really, no more deaths. I love you so much. Please don't go." He holds and kisses her hand. "Why does fate always have to separate us?" says Josh.

The paramedics are struggling to keep her pulse. They arrive at Citywide Hospital. Josh gets out. They rush Linda to the emergency room. One of the nurses stops him and says, "It would be best if you waited in the waiting room, sir."

"I can't," Josh says. As he tries to move past her, she stops him again.

"Please, sir," the nurse says.

"Okay . . . okay," Josh says. In the waiting room, he calls Linda's parents, Samantha, and Eric to tell them what happened. The worst phone call is to the parents; the crying and the sound of ripping hearts stabs him.

Twenty minutes later, Josh can see Linda's family, Eric, and Samantha rushing down the hall. Josh explains what happened. After two hours or so a six-foot-two male doctor named Wiser walks up to them.

"Are you the Cresswood family?" Dr. Wiser asks.

"Yes, how's my daughter?" asks Mrs. Cresswood desperately.

The doctor takes a deep breath. "Your daughter, Linda Cresswood . . . did not make it. I am sorry. We tried everything, but she was losing too much blood and the damage to her internal organs was extensive. She passed away."

After he finishes his sentence, it's as if a bomb explodes. Mr. and Mrs. Cresswood break down into tears. Linda's brother David cries uncontrollably. "What? My sister can't be dead," says David as he continues to cry. Samantha faints. Josh runs out of the hospital. Eric leaves the building to chase after Josh.

The doctor leaves them to deal with their emotions. The other nurses try to help Samantha regain consciousness. Seven minutes later, Samantha wakes up from being unconscious. "Why are there elephants in this hospital? Why is everything so loud? The colors are too bright. Now I have a ghost friend," Samantha says as she giggles to herself. She begins to laugh hysterically.

"What are you saying? Is everything okay? Are you okay?" asks the nurse.

"Why would I be okay if I don't have my doll?" says Samantha as she slaps the nurse across her face. The other nurse calls security. They quickly arrive on the scene. Samantha gets even more out of control.

"No, you can't arrest the princess fairy," Samantha screams as they drag her out of the waiting room. "I'll turn you all into toads." She laughs frenziedly. "Nobody's safe from the evil witch," says Samantha as she cries and laughs at the same time "Linda's fine, Jennifer's fine . . . everyone's alive and happy. Let me go. I have to meet them by the rainbow for a picnic!" Samantha yells as she struggles to get loose. She starts to scratch her face and body while at the same time trying to scratch and bite other people. Samantha's face bleeds. She smears her blood around her face and clothes then vomits on the floor.

The Cresswoods see security drag her away. This only makes them cry harder. Some people in the hospital stop what they are doing for a second because they can hear Samantha's screams echoing down the hall.

Chapter Thirty-Seven

I want to die to live again.
I want to be everything that
I prevented myself from being.
Io, il sobillatore. (I, the troublemaker.)

Eric and Josh run like the wind. Somehow Eric manages to catch up to Josh and grab his arm.

"Where are you going?" demands Eric.

"Leave me the fuck alone!" screams Josh as he wrestles out of Eric's grip.

"This is not the way to deal with this," says Eric.

"You don't know me. Why do you even care?" asks Josh.

"You're my friend, and I know how much you liked Linda. I could tell by the way you looked at her," says Eric.

"You're wrong, I didn't like her . . . I loved her. Don't you fucking understand, Eric? She finally decided to be my girlfriend. I am her boyfriend. You don't know anything. Don't you see that everyone we care about is dying around us?" says Josh.

Josh's sudden burst of truth and emotion surprises Eric. "You didn't tell me . . . I . . . know what you're feeling because it hurt the same way when Jenny died. I . . . know this is very heavy . . . but you have to pull through this. I don't think that either Jennifer or Linda would want us to fall apart like this."

"I don't want to listen to your fucking advice," says Josh as he runs off again.

Eric does not stop him. He just can't. He watches Josh run, his body a silhouette against the afternoon sun. Eric thinks about what Josh said. *He's right. Everything is falling apart. Jennifer was a beautiful person full of excitement. She shined and was amazing. Why did that have to happen to Jenny? What about Linda? She was enchanting. She had a spark in her that just made you feel so good.* Eric smiles as he remembers the good times. *Linda was addicting. I feel so empty. Linda helped me so much, and Jennifer made me laugh when I felt down. I can't believe these wonderful people are gone. I don't want to think about this anymore.* Eric starts to walk home. He begins to cry because he has lost everything . . . .

Josh storms into his room in a fit of rage. He completely trashes his room, breaking, throwing, and destroying everything until he gets tired. He falls to the floor and begins to cry. *Society says it's not manly for a guy to cry, but I don't give a shit about who wants to control me right now.* He sits on the floor as he cries more heavily. *This can't be possible,* Josh thinks. *How could something this horrible happen in one person's life? I will not be able to feel her, listen to her, make love to her, or breathe her in.* The pain feels unbearable. *I want to torture the people responsible for this, and after they suffer the amount of pain they caused her, me, and everybody else, I will then kill them. I hate everything and just want to kill everybody. I can't imagine my life without Linda, not even if I try.* His thoughts are not processing right now. Josh cannot handle all these volatile emotions. *I have to do something to dull the impact . . . .*

Eric calmly walks into his empty house and then walks up to his room and sits in his chair. He stares at the white painted walls as he contemplates all the events that have occurred. *I loved Jennifer and Linda for different reasons. I loved their different personalities. The question is, whom do I love more, Linda or Jennifer? The answer is simple. Linda. Linda was always there for me. She had a heavenly, lovely, beautiful quality. That sparked my desires. I never even had a chance to really fall in love with Jennifer or get to know her more personally than as a friend. Jennifer was beautiful, and funny. She made people feel happy. Nevertheless, I never felt the raw emotions that I had with Linda when I was around Jennifer. I feel like a horrible person. I don't want to make one girl seem better than the other. However, this is how I feel. I really deeply cared about Jennifer, and her death affected me profoundly. But Linda's death now, as well? This is something I will never and cannot cope with.* "Fuck! Linda, maybe it was you who I really wanted for a girlfriend and so much more. Yes, I'm going to admit it. Deep in my subconscious I know it's true. Why am I such a fucking rotten bastard? I'm so demented that I didn't know which woman I truly loved. Jennifer? Samantha? I'm sorry I involved you guys in my confusion. It was you, Linda, who I wanted the whole time." He sighs. "Linda, you're my soul mate, my life vest. Who's going to listen to my complaining now?" says Eric as he laughs lightly. He tries to ease the heavy tension that hangs in the air.

Eric opens the bottom drawer of his desk. He takes out a white shoebox. He removes the cloth. He pulls out a gun, a 9-millimeter. He got it after his eighteenth birthday. Sometimes, he likes to practice shooting. The gun feels cold and smooth, a lot like life. Eric also takes out the bullets that came with it. He loads the gun to its capacity and then closes it up. He clicks the safety off. Eric then points the gun at his temple. He goes to pull the trigger. A burst of memory pops into his head and stalls him. He remembers a conversation with Linda. *Wait, I remember now. What did she ask me? I remember now. She made me promise her that I would never kill myself. I remember that now. I promised her. I remember her telling me that it would hurt her.* He lowers the gun. *I have to keep that sacred. It is a bond that connects her to me. It's a long distance one that is between the worlds we now occupy. I cannot let her down. Alive or dead, I would never want to hurt her.*

Eric sets the gun down. He takes out the bullets from the gun, clicks the safety back on, and puts everything away. This whole time he is quite calm. Eric buries his face in his arms and weeps on his desk.

Chapter Thirty-Eight

Josh calls up some people who are on the shady side. He knows them, but has not talked to them for a while because he knew he was only going to find trouble if he kept hanging out with them. But they did know how to have a good time. Josh did not give a shit. *Tonight, I want to get drunk and high, and if there are some girls . . . why not?*

He drives over to their house. There is loud music, and many people. Josh greets his old friends. They are waiting outside. He takes the alcohol offered to him, and they go into the house and upstairs into a room. When they open the door, there is a haze of marijuana. Some people in the corner are snorting crack.

"So, Joshua . . . ," says Leroy. Leroy never finished high school. He came from a rich Dominican family. He is six feet, has a muscular build, and he is a drug dealer. Josh met him during his first year in high school when they were studying auto mechanics. The rest of the people in the room are addicts, delinquents, and lost people, destroyed by their own vices. Josh knew some of them. He remembered what they looked like when they were good people.

"Have a seat, Josh. It's been awhile," says Leroy.

"Yeah, it has," says Josh.

"So how you been?" asks Mavi.

"Okay, just enjoying the summer," says Josh.

Mavi came from a poor, abusive Mexican family. Josh met him too in auto shop class. All three of them helped each other out to pass that class. The only reason Mavi was able to go to a school full of rich white kids was through a special program for underprivileged kids. He is five-eight and muscular too. He is now one of the head members of a notorious gang in some ghetto barrio outside of town and away from the suburbs. He does his thing out there, in the merciless big city.

Leroy and Mavi work together on the drug deals. Mavi's gang protects and distributes for Leroy's business. Leroy, in exchange, offers a supply and plans. In return for money, too, of course. They are both extremely handsome, but savagely dangerous.

I remember how smart Mavi was and how he used to dream of getting a scholarship in soccer so that he could go to a high-quality university. I guess he changed his mind, Josh thinks.

"*Oye cabron, por qué no nos llamaste?*" (Hey asshole, why didn't you call us.) asks Mavi.

"*No se, me olvidé porque estaba distraido por las pendejadas de mi vida. Asi es la pinche vida, no?*"

(I don't know, I was distracted by the stupid shit in my life. That's fucking life, right?") replies Josh.

"*Asi es,*" (That's how it is.) replies Mavi.

Josh knows how to speak Spanish because he comes from a mixed family.

"*Basta con las preguntas,* okay? *Josh no tiene que explicar nada a nosotros. La cosa importante es que él está aquí,*" (Enough with the questioning, okay? Josh doesn't have to explain anything to us. The important thing is that he is here.) says Leroy as he snorts some coke.

"Can I have some?" asks Josh.

"This shit ain't cheap, but since you're a friend, it's okay," says Leroy.

Josh lines it and snorts it up using a crisp hundred-dollar bill. It feels as if something exploded in his mind. Mavi takes out his and snorts it up too. They start talking about the past and stupid stuff.

After an hour of laughing and talking, some slutty chicks walk into the room.

"Hey, Josh. This is Rachel, Vanessa, and Olivia," says Leroy.

"Hi, baby," says Rachel to Josh. She is obviously drunk. She walks over to him and sits on his lap. Vanessa starts to make out with Leroy, and Olivia begins to make out with Mavi. The rest of the people in the room are either passed out or making out with someone.

"Rachel, that's a nice name," says Josh. He is very high. Josh and Rachel begin making out. After ten minutes, she passes out. Josh pushes her aside and stands up.

"Hey, Josh," says Leroy. Leroy walks over to him and pulls out some ecstasy tablets that were in his pocket. "I just got some new product. Try it out for me. I got to keep my shit good for the customers," Leroy explains. He offers them to Josh. Josh takes one. Mavi whines for one too. Leroy gives in and gives him one. Leroy doesn't try the ecstasy himself though.

"So how much do I have to pay you?" asks Josh.

"Don't you worry about that. It's free because I like you," says Leroy with a crocodile smile.

"Okay," says Josh. The world begins to spin around him. Josh, Leroy. and Mavi begin talking again. They are all wasted and high, talking about nonsense and laughing a whole lot.

After some hours, Josh can tell the party is over. "I have to go. It's late," says Josh as he gets up.

"*Adios, compa.* (Bye, my friend.) See you around," says Mavi.

"*Nos vemos,*" (See you later.) says Leroy. They all do their bro handshake and hug as Josh says bye.

When Josh walks out the door, he can see that Leroy and Mavi are taking their girls into separate bedrooms. *I wonder where Rachel went,* Josh thinks. He gets into his car anyway. *This is not a good idea. I'm high,* Josh thinks as he turns on the ignition. He also thinks about his parents. *I don't care if my parents wonder where I am. I need some fresh air.*

Chapter Thirty-Nine

I've come to the realization that my destiny lies in ruins.
I'm so tired of the light and dark that it now burns
my eyes. I can cry forever and still not be safe.

"Please someone try to control her!" yells a doctor. Samantha thrashes about.

"Can we get some help in here?" demands a nurse. Some heavyset guards try to calm her down. They carry her to an empty room and put her on the cold, generic, hospital bed. They pin her down.

"Where's the damn shot?" asks the doctor.

"I got it right here," yells another nurse, running toward them from the hall. She passes the materials over to the doctor, who fills the syringe with a chemical of submission.

"Hold her down," yells the doctor. The doctor injects her.

Samantha feels her emotions drain. She starts to feel dizzy. "I remember everything. Just kill me, please," says Samantha in a low voice before she passes out . . . .

Josh drives up to Point Sands. Miraculously, he does not get into an accident driving there. When he gets out of the car, it revitalizes his system. The wind feels amazing. He walks toward the cliffs. The soft gravel scrunches against his feet as he walks. He looks around. The area feels sacred. *I want to forget everything. Everything feels so stupid and frustrating right now. No matter how hard I try, the memories keep coming back.* "Shut up!" yells Josh as he put his hands on his head.

Josh thinks about Linda. *I feel like everything is spinning, I feel like I am going insane. I'm beginning to see things. Is that Linda? Standing by the trees? She looks as beautiful as ever.* He begins to laugh. One could either cry or laugh during a struggle. Josh's mind is going in several directions. *I wish she were right next to me. I loved her free spirit.*

"Linda, you're with me forever. Even in death I can see your pretty face. A goddess for a peasant," Josh says.

He is now in a state of delirium. "You showed me how to explore the hidden part of life where logic doesn't exist and only fantasy and creativity reign. You made me let go of my materialistic possessions to become one with the earth and let my inner child live again. Summer belongs to us now. The music of our souls runs though the blood in our veins. I want to celebrate the lives of our ancestors. Let us ride our horses into battle and destroy the enemy called civilization. Let us become savage once more. Let the heavens come down and fill us with power, so that you will be my lover for eternity. Nothing can kill us because we belong to the spirits now!" Josh screams as he laughs and stumbles around.

The bad E, the coke, and the alcohol are getting to him. "Linda . . . why did you abandon me!" Josh screams, his voice echoing through the darkness.

He looks at the stars. It looks as if they have exploded across the sky. The air rushes past him and through him. *I feel so alive. I feel Linda's presence. I strangely feel at peace. Everything looks so beautiful.* The trees rustle through the wind. Josh walks up to the edge of the cliff. It is really far down below. The ocean looks so deep, like a dark mass of mystery. The waves sound like thunder as they crash against the rocks. *I want to breathe in her soul once more.* His brain is working in fragments. "Memories fall and surround me. Inhaling as I exhale. Beats . . . surrounded. Madness has consumed me and has become one with me. I do not exist anymore. It blurs the vision. I hear crying, laughing, and loving. You are everything to me, and I am your nothing. Linda, you took a piece of my soul. Functioning normally is obsolete."

Josh takes a deep breath and closes his eyes "Now, I finally feel at peace . . . actually happy . . . with you," he whispers. Tears are streaming down his face. He jumps off the cliff. The action is swift and quiet, a non-disturbance of the earth. It occurs organically.

His lifeless body will eventually wash up on the shore in the morning. It is reported in the local newspaper. The reactions of Josh's parents are pain, devastation, and sadness. Their emotions are words that explain themselves, but never at what depth.

The quiet suburban town becomes a town of many funerals. Samantha spends her days in psychiatric care, paid for her by her parents, who are desperate to make her feel better. They constantly cry and blame themselves for what she has become.

Samantha enjoys spending her time talking to herself. It may look like that to other people, but to Samantha she is having a normal conversation with her friends Linda and Jennifer. Samantha is in solitary confinement because she is a danger to other patients. She has stopped eating and sleeping. She has to wear a straitjacket to avoid disfiguring herself and injuring others around her. She likes to spend her days rocking back and forth, back and forth.

Eric couldn't cope with all the events, so he took some necessities and left town. His parents read his "runaway" note. They got worried out of their minds and called the police to try to locate him. No one knows where he went, but hopefully it is very far away.

Rodney, Jeff, and Will get drug charges. But Will, the driver of the Ferrari, gets vehicular manslaughter tacked on to his sentence.

Since the prosecutors could not have Linda's testimony for Jennifer's trial, they used the eyewitness accounts at the club instead. The witnesses decided to come forward due to the police asking for help on the news.

The man responsible for Jennifer's death and rape is John Verna. He is twenty-six, a drug user who works at a factory. He also has a record of petty crimes and assault. The reason the cops could not match his DNA to his profile in the beginning was due to a glitch in the system.

Sometimes life can be ridiculous. Anyway, you cannot see John's way of life just by looking at him. This is because appearances lie and deceive. The bright lights of the courtroom do expose his unhealthy aspect caused by continued drug use. The DNA they got from him came back as a perfect match for the semen, fingerprints, and other DNA found at the crime scene.

The jury finds him guilty on the charge of involuntary manslaughter and rape. He shows no physical reaction. His eyes just get watery. They take him away.

Jennifer's parents and brother are relieved and happy as they cry together.

It is a beautiful day. It is sunny, not a cloud in the sky. You can hear the echoing of birds chirping and the buzzing of insects.